Forewarned . . .

Chiun gave Remo a polished jade inscribed with three Korean characters. ''Your opponents all have similar stones,'' he said. ''They will find you through it.''

Remo read the characters. ''The Brotherhood,'' he read. ''I thought these guys were supposed to be my enemies.''

''Perhaps you will learn something of enmity and friendship on this journey,'' Chiun said as Remo got into the boat.

''There's just one thing before I go. In the scroll you sent me, it said something—''

''The Other,'' H'si T'ang said. He sniffed the ocean air. ''He is coming. Beware.''

Chiun looked at H'si T'ang. ''Who is he, my teacher?''

''I cannot see. But someone close, very close. His spirit is near. We are deceived. The Other is of two beings. Yin and yang . . .'' His words drifted off, and H'si T'ang shook his head rapidly. ''The vision is gone.''

''The Other,'' Remo mused. ''A fifth opponent?''

''I do not know who he is, only that he comes.''

''For me?'' Remo asked.

''He is coming for all of us.''

THE DESTROYER SERIES:

A SUPERNOVEL

The Destroyer #55

Warren Murphy & Richard Sapir

MASTER'S CHALLENGE

PINNACLE BOOKS NEW YORK

DESTROYER #55: MASTER'S CHALLENGE

Copyright © 1984 by Warren Murphy and Richard Sapir

An original Pinnacle Books edition, published for the first time anywhere.

First printing, February 1984

ISBN: 0-523-41565-6

Can. ISBN: 0-523-43100-7

Cover illustration by Hector Garrido

Printed in the United States of America

PINNACLE BOOKS, INC.
1430 Broadway
New York, New York 10018

9 8 7 6 5 4 3 2 1

For the harmonica player, and the Glorious House of Sinanju, P.O. Box 1454, Secaucus, N.J. 07094

Prologue

The Legend

It came to pass that the great assassin Wang, first Master of the glorious house of Sinanju, came to be known and admired the world over for his feats of strength and agility and discipline of mind. But there were those, far away among the wild peoples of the earth, who questioned the Master's power and challenged him to test his strength against their own.

The Master, in his wisdom, knew that these peoples, whose diverse civilizations were as ancient as his own, were not his enemies, but his equals. For amid all the timid hordes of men who lived lives of sloth and insignificance, only these few remained from the ancient days of glory and kept the traditions and secrets of their ancestors. Thus deeming them to be worthy opponents, the Master accepted their challenge.

He traveled to each of their lands in succession, carrying neither arms nor food, and met with the best among them in mortal combat. Although his opponents fought with honor and courage, the Master vanquished them all, bowing after each death and commending to the gods the departed spirits of his fallen adversaries.

When he had slain the last of his opponents, the family and friends of the dead man fell upon Wang in anger. But the Master spoke, saying, "Do not seek to make war on me, for we are not among those people who annihilate without thought. We are few in the world, we of valor and faith in the ancient ways. Let us leave one another in peace."

"My son will be avenged," spoke the father of the slain warrior.

The Master of Sinanju answered him, saying, "Then prepare your son's son to do battle with my successor. And for each generation after, let our best meet together in blood for the ultimate test of their powers. We shall be enemies but once in a lifetime. For all the rest of our days, may we leave one another in privacy and peace."

Thus was the beginning of the secret ritual known as the Master's Trial.

MASTER'S CHALLENGE

Chapter One

Ancion paused at the end of Kwasha Challa, the sacred rope bridge that separated his domain from the rest of Peru. Kwasha Challa had been built just for him, specifically for this crossing, as an identical bridge had been built a generation ago for his father.

Twelve hundred feet below, the Apurimac river boiled with white rapids. Beyond it lay the green Peruvian highlands dotted with the ancient burial towers of Ancion's ancestors. It would be, he knew, some time before he saw them again.

The oracle had predicted a safe journey for him. Still, it was one he did not look forward to making. He would have to cross most of the known world, alone and penniless as tradition decreed, to reach the place his people called the Land at the End of the World. From the accounts given by his father and grandfather, it was a desolate place, cold and inhospitable, with rocks in place of the lush and startling contrasts of his native land.

He mounted the white llama that had been left for him. His father had done the same. And his grandfather, dressed

1

in the same kind of garments that Ancion now wore, the woven *wincha* wound around his head for warmth, the silver pin holding his cloak together, and the large gold discs pierced into his ears that communicated to those who understood that Ancion was an Inca, *the* Inca, reigning king of a people believed by the world to be long extinguished.

For when Pizarro looted the Inca Empire in 1532 and murdered Atahualpa, the "last" Inca, his band of blood-thirsty Spaniards missed an enclave in the mountains where Ancion's ancestors ruled. Since then, Ancion's people had lived, hidden and secret, away from the ways of other men. Only one Inca in each generation, *the* Inca, was permitted to leave, and then only on two occasions. The first was a stay in the outside world to learn its ways in order to better protect his people from them. The second time was to make the journey Ancion was embarking on now, the journey to meet the most powerful being on earth. It was a tradition not to be questioned.

In his pockets were some dried potatoes, the precious *papa* that had sustained his people for 5,000 years, and his weapon. It was a *bola*, a cord weighted by a rock en-crusted with sharp stones. Used properly, it was deadly enough to kill a cougar in flight. The bola and a small sharp knife at his waist were Ancion's only defenses against the white and black and yellow men who stood between him and his destiny. They would be enough.

Unwinding the cord carefully, he whirled the bola over his head until it sang. Then he lowered it, still vibrating in his hands, and snapped the two thick ropes that bound the bridge to the land. Kwasha Challa fell, destroying the only entrance into his country until his return. It was done. His journey had begun.

The journey to Sinanju. The Land at the End of the World.

*   *   *

Emrys ap Llewellyn fastened his knapsack around his huge, square shoulders. "Griffith!" he called.

"Up here, Da," a small voice rang from the top of a tall pine. It echoed through the green hills surrounding the valley. The boy laughed as the big man made a show of stalking the tree like a bear. With both hands gripping the pine's trunk, Emrys shook it. The boy fell out of the branches into his arms, shrieking with delight.

"Got you now," Emrys said, hugging his son. The boy's hair smelled of pine and deep woods.

"Do it again, Da."

"That I cannot." Emrys hitched up his knapsack again. "It's time I'll be going, son."

Griffith's face fell. His large, soft eyes welled with tears.

"Now, none of your caterwauling. It's time, and that's that. Go on to home, you shameful baby."

"But Da, your eyes—"

"Don't you be talking back to me, scamp!" He swatted the boy across the bottom.

"Don't go, Da," Griffith wailed. "You'll not see well enough to fight the Chinee. He'll kill you sure."

Emrys turned on him fiercely. "I'll not have you speaking so to your old father."

His eyes were different from his son's. For all their understanding, they were warrior's eyes, and Griffith's words stopped at the sight of them. But he couldn't stop the tears. "It ain't right, so it's not," the boy said miserably.

"You've just got to understand. This is something I've got to do. It's the way of our kin. One day you'll be going, too."

"I don't want to fight the damned Chinee," the boy protested.

"Watch your mouth!"

"I want to stay here, in these woods, with the Old Ones, the spirits. And I want you to stay with me. Now that Ma's gone, we're all we have, you and me."

Emrys cleared his throat. Sometimes Griffith sounded as if he were a hundred years old. "Well, what a man wants and what he's got to do are two different things," he said gruffly. "Besides, your Ma made you promise on the day she died to mind me. Did you not promise her?"

The boy stared at the ground.

"Did you na?"

"Yes. I promised."

"Then go home. And not another word."

Emrys stomped off toward the hills, following the winding stream that bisected the valley. It had been a raging river once, in the days when all of Wales was as wild and unknown as the valley and its surrounding woods.

There were no roads here, no electricity, no running water. No taxes, no trolleys, no army. Instead, there were the hills, still dotted with the ancient shrines of gods who had been worshiped before the Romans came. Mryddin, oldest among the dieties, still ruled in the valley. There was the forest, still populated with the wild, savvy people who had dwelled there since the beginning of time, where the great magician Merlin himself had hidden while he waited for young King Arthur to come of age.

There were spirits and music and timeless enchantment in the valley; outside was the contamination of the new world. And beyond that, far off in lands so distant and strange that Emrys could not even imagine them from the stories his father, Llewellyn, had told him, were other knots of civilization that still clung to the old, true ways.

The place where he was going was one of those. The people there were fighters, like Emrys's own kind. The Masters of Sinanju were rarely bested in battle. Llewellyn himself had fallen at the hands of the great Chinee. It had been a terrible shock to Emrys, who was already fully grown by the time his father took on the Master of Sinanju. The Chinee was a small, weak-looking man well past middle age. But Llewellyn had explained after his return from Sinanju, while he waited for the Master to come do battle with him, that the people of that land lived so far away that even their appearance was different. Their size had little to do with their strength, and their peculiar slanted eyes could see the legs on a caterpillar at twenty paces.

As his father lay dead, Emrys had been tempted to attack the frail-looking Oriental himself. But the Chinee who had killed Llewellyn did an odd thing in his moment of victory. He found Emrys in the crowd of onlookers and bowed to him. The look in the Master's hazel eyes had not been one of triumph, but of respect for Emrys's dead father. Llewellyn had fought well, and the Master of Sinanju had acknowledged his valor. It was during that moment that Emrys came to understand the Master's Trial, and why his people had honored the contest since the days when the river ran wide as an ocean through the valley. The outcome of the Trial was final. Until now.

It was Emrys's turn, at last, to challenge the protegee of the Master of Sinanju and avenge Llewellyn's death. Once in each generation. It was his only opportunity.

He squeezed his eyes shut hard, as if the movement would disperse the cloudiness of his vision. Of course, it didn't work. It never did. He only hoped his sight would hold out long enough for him to do the things he had to do: go to Sinanju to meet with the great Chinee in peace. Return to the valley to prepare for battle. Encounter the Master's son when he arrived in Wales. And kill him.

There was another thing he had to do as well, and the thought filled Emrys with worry. He had to prepare Griffith to fight in his own generation's Master's Trial. For regardless of the outcome of this contest, Griffith would have to go forth to the next.

What had happened to Griffith? Emrys's people sprang from fighting stock that went back for thousands of years. Now here was his own son, Griffith ap Emrys, who could not even bring himself to kill a squirrel. Emrys had come to blows more than once in defense of the boy whom the others labeled weak and girlish, but there was no denying it: Griffith was a sad excuse for a warrior. While the other boys of the valley practiced their falls and developed their fists on one another, Griffith spent all his time exploring the old altars of the dead gods, so long vanished that even the forest people did not remember their names. He raised lost birds and sang made-up songs into the air. He slept, frequently, in caves thick with bats and did not fear even the wildest horse. But he would not fight.

Perhaps it was the lack of a mother. Emrys's wife Brawnwyn had died so young.

He turned for a last look at his home. The valley, stretching below him, looked like a miasma of diffused light. *Just let my eyes hold out*, he said to himself. In the center of the dim, velvet-toned valley stood Griffith where Emrys had left him.

"What will become of my strange little child?" he asked the wind. He waved slowly to the small figure and then turned away, before he could think of an answer.

Jilda guided the slender wooden boat expertly over the freezing swells of the Bering Strait. On either side of her rose the continents of Asia and America, vast lands filled with decaying, soft men and uselessly ornamental women.

She was hungry. Keeping one oar in motion, she pulled a long iron-tipped spear from the bottom of the boat. The water was rough. Jilda stood up in the tossing boat, watching. She saw a flash of silver, poised her spear, then lowered it, cursing. A halibut, but too big. Its weight would capsize the boat. She waited, immobile, perfectly balanced on the choppy waves.

Her ancestors had watched and waited in exactly the same way, standing in the narrow-hulled boats that carried the first of the Vikings to glory in the weak lands that stood like ripe fruit ready for picking. The Norsemen who had carried the lightning of Thor from Norway throughout Europe and Russia a thousand years ago had waited with their spears in the air and hunger gnawing at their bellies just as Jilda did now.

She felt their blood in her. She was proud, because her forefathers were the purest of the magnificent warriors who had ruled the sea. When the Viking conquest drew to a close, most of her people changed and adapted. They learned to live at peace with the world. They accepted lives of comfort and idleness. But her own people, the small knot of sea-toughened men and women who had refused to lose their wildness and their instinct for survival, chose to leave their homeland instead.

Many Vikings settled in the remote Faeroes Islands deep in the Norwegian Sea, and her ancestors were among these. But her people, sensing the pervading onslaught of modern ways even to this distant archipelago, chose to separate themselves from the rest of their kind. They selected for their new home the smallest, coldest land mass in the Faeroes chain, an uninhabited island that they named Lakluun. And on Lakluun they fished and hunted, built their turf-covered stone croft houses, brewed mead from fermented honey, praised their gods, revered their legends, burned their dead at sea, raised their young, and survived with the old ways.

A flutter on the surface of the water. The fish was a young one, its two flat eyes flashing in the sunlight on its right side. Halibut. Effortlessly, Jilda tossed in her spear and rowed to catch it before it sank. She cut the still-moving flesh with the dagger she carried in her belt and ate it raw.

Where was this place she was going? The elders had told her nothing, except that she was to meet a great warrior and challenge his son in battle. The contest was called the Master's Trial. Why it was necessary to determine a master among races of people who had no earthly contact with one another had puzzled her, but the elders did not speak of it.

It was the way things were done. As the best fighter on Lakluun, it was Jilda's duty to comply, just as it had been her duty to kill the first of the beasts offered during the Sacrifice of Nine. The animals were not used for food but for ceremony, and the ceremony sickened her. Once every nine years the people of Lakluun offered the sacrifice to Thor, Odin, and Freya, the three gods of thunder, war, and pleasure, killing nine of every male creature in existence and displaying them in the Sacred Wood for the deities to see. For weeks, the gentle woods stank with the corpses of horses hanging by their necks next to the maggot-covered bodies of dogs and reindeer. But nothing was so terrible as the sight of the nine hanged men, stolen from wayward fishing boats, their eyes rotting and blistered beneath the trees.

Tradition. How she despised the elders' senseless traditions! It was horrifying to kill nine innocent men for the delight of the gods, but that was what tradition decreed. And it was contemptible to journey halfway around the world to meet a warrior for the purpose of killing not the warrior himself, but his *son*, whom she had never even seen. Tradition? Bah. It was stupidity, insanity, waste!

But then, without tradition, where would her people be? Living the lives of slugs hiding in shells, crawling for their every need? What would Jilda herself be without the strength and spirit of her ancestors? A fat, dimpled wife, perhaps, screaming at infants and driving a padded automobile with rubber tires? A cooperative worker, running in her rat's maze each day without a mouthful of clear air, devoid of freedom or dignity?

No, she would choose death rather than submit to the life of the world outside Lakluun. But was there no way to avoid the disgusting practice of the Master's Trial?

Jilda finished her meal and threw the bones overboard. She wiped her hands on the leather cape she wore over her long grown. Her pale eyes changed color, as they did when she was deep in thought. She had a plan.

She would meet with the Master of Sinanju as tradition demanded. She was the chosen warrior of Lakluun, and it was her right to speak with the Master and the other contestants. When she did speak, she would tell them all to abandon the Trial. Surely none of them wished to kill a perfect stranger in the name of some foolish contest. This was one tradition that had to be stopped. And if she could stop it, she could return to Lakluun and end forever the Sacrifice of Nine.

She picked up her oars again, satisfied.

Kiree was cold, colder than he had ever been in his life. The occasional soldiers he spotted along the rocky shores of the place called Sinanju posed no problem; he was dark and small and accustomed to hiding and moving quickly. He had not been confronted by a single human during his entire journey.

But the weather, even in May, would surely kill him. In the Dogon region of central Mali, where his people, the Tellem, lived, temperatures of 115 degrees were not unusual. The heat could be withstood, but the cold . . . Who could live in such a frozen wasteland? During his long trip, Kiree had at times considered wearing protective clothing, as others native to the frigid area did, but he had discarded the idea. He was a Tellem. He would wear the loose black cotton leg wrappers of his people, the white cotton cap, the string of antelope teeth around his neck, the ceremonial red sash around his waist, and nothing more. If he could not stand the cold, then he deserved to die ignominiously before his turn at battle.

He made his way carefully toward the cave, moving quickly in the night shadows. Before his death at the hands of the yellow man, the great warrior Balpa Dolo had described the cave to Kiree.

"It is the home of the ancients of the Yellow Land," Balpa Dolo had said. "Outside the entrance are plants that have not been seen in all of Africa. Three plants, a pine, a bamboo, and a plum blossom. But you will not need this sign. The cave is a holy place, and you will feel its holiness. Open your senses, and your instinct will take you there."

Kiree had closed his eyes at the shore of Sinanju, and felt and listened for the thrum of life. He felt it only weakly from ordinary humans, but among the Tellem, the vibration was strong. And here, too, the unheard music of concentrated, instinctual life pulled him toward the cave and nowhere else. He did not see the flowers until he was almost at the mouth of the hill.

A thin old man with strange features and golden skin emerged from the cave on footsteps so silent and controlled that even the dust beneath his feet did not move. He wore a robe of dazzling red, embroidered with threads that shimmered like water in sunlight. He was small, nearly as small as Kiree, and looked as insubstantial as a feather. To Kiree's eyes, the yellow man resembled nothing as much as a series of high clouds, from the wispy white hair on his head and chin to the slender, inch-long fingernails on his hands. And yet there was power about him. Near him, the thrum of life was deafening to Kiree's sensitive instincts. And there was peace, too, the unmistakable serenity of the born warrior.

"You are the Master of Sinanju," Kiree said in English.

The frail-looking old Korean bowed formally. "I am Chiun," he said. "I welcome you to this place of peace."

Inside the cave, the vibrant life force washed over Kiree like warm waves. The other contestants sat on a fragrant grass mat that covered the floor, their faces bright in the light from a smokeless fire. There was an enormous white man, a thin, aristocratic brown man with a high-bridged nose and jewels in his ears, and a woman with golden hair. The level of energy that emanated from them was almost tangible. The cave was alive with pure life. Balpa Dolo had been right. It was a holy place.

"There is safety here," he said softly.

The splendidly robed Oriental smiled. "There is always safety among persons of honor."

Chiun brought food and drink, and treated each of the guests with impeccable courtesy. "Now that you have all assembled here, I wish you to meet another of my people," he said.

"Your son?" Emrys asked.

"No. According to the rules of the Master's Trial, the protegee of the victor does not meet with the challengers before the hour of combat. At the appointed time, my son will travel to your lands, just as you have come to Sinanju, alone. This is a meeting of peace among those of us who have kept the old ways in the face of the new."

"The old ways are not always the best ways," Jilda said. Her voice was respectful, but her chin was thrust out defiantly.

Ancion's dark eyes flashed. "Do you mean to lead your people away from their traditions?" He looked at Jilda with contempt.

"I speak only of the Master's Trial. It is a tradition that is unworthy of us."

Ancion set down his bowl with distaste and rose quickly. As he did, he stepped on the hem of his cloak, momentarily losing his balance. He broke his fall with his hands, digging into the red-hot peat of the fire. Ancion yelped with the pain, righting himself. "You do not belong here!" he spat.

"And you are only angry because you have shamed yourself by tripping over your clothes like a child," Jilda taunted.

"Hold. Hold." The voice, thin and quavering, came from deep within the recesses of the cave. The contestants fell silent as they watched an old, old man emerge from the shadows. He was heavyset and bald, and his face was so worn and wrinkled that it looked like a crumpled sheet of translucent parchment, but he held his back perfectly straight. His eyes were like those of a statue, their pupils pale and unseeing.

Emrys rose. "The old Master," he said. The others murmured. "My father spoke of you. The most powerful of all the Masters of Sinanju."

"The Venerable One," Jilda said. "I remember, too. It is he of the Sight."

"H'si T'ang," Kiree whispered. "The warrior who can see the future."

"I would much rather see the present," the old man said, smiling. "But these eyes have long since abandoned this old body." He turned his sightless gaze toward the fire.

Chiun took his hand. "H'si T'ang was my teacher," he said, helping the old man to a place at the fire beside Ancion. The Inca regarded him coldly.

"And who are you, my children?" H'si T'ang asked.

"If you have the Sight, you should know who we are," Ancion said.

Jilda slapped the floor with her open palm. "How dare you speak to the Venerable One in this way!"

"Venerable One," Ancion mocked. "A useless blind man who lives in a cave."

The others protested, but H'si T'ang quieted them. "Ancion may speak as he likes here." He turned to the Inca. "You are quite right, my son. It is to a shamefully inadequate dwelling that Chiun has brought you, but it was for a reason. You see, the Master of Sinanju occupies, by tradition, a house in the village, but Chiun believed that you would prefer to meet in secrecy. That is why he chose my home for this gathering. He did not intend to insult you by bringing you here."

"It is a holy place," Kiree said. "The cave where our fathers met."

"You remember well," H'si T'ang said.

"It's good enough for me," Emrys added belligerently.

"It is still a cave," Ancion said flatly. "And I would like to know why the so-called Master of Sinanju allows his teacher to live in such a rough place. In my homeland, when the old king passes on his powers to the new, he continues to live in splendor. It is his due. You seem to me a man worthy of little respect among your own people."

H'si T'ang smiled. "At my age, respect from one's peers is not so important as understanding of one's own heart. This 'rough place,' as you call it, is of my own choosing. For it is here, away from the traffic of daily life, that I may contemplate all the things that I was too busy to notice during my youth." He reached for the Inca's long, tapering fingers. "For example, twenty years ago, I would not have been able to know that your hands were burned without seeing or touching you."

Ancion snatched his hands away. "Don't touch me."

"I am more than one hundred and thirty years old," H'si T'ang said. "I would not harm you, but I can help you." With an impossibly swift motion, he clapped Ancion's hands between his own and held them. When he released them, the Inca stared at his palms in amazement. The burns had healed completely in the instant that H'si T'ang had touched them.

"Sorcery," Ancion whispered, making a sign against witchcraft. "One such as you should never have been permitted to fight in the Master's Trial. You killed my grandfather with trickery."

"I felled your grandfather, the great warrior Huaton, in combat."

"You bewitched him!" Ancion shrieked.

"I cannot bewitch. I can only heal. I would have healed Huaton if I could, but he was dead even before he fell."

Ancion shouted him down. "There is no Master's Trial, only the work of sorcerers!"

"Stop it!" Jilda commanded. "The Master's Trial is an evil thing. It is causing us to turn against one another already."

"This is not your affair, woman," Ancion said coldly.

"I am one of the contestants in this misbegotten game, and it *is* my affair," Jilda said. "We must stop the Trial before it begins. There are so few of us left, we people of honor and strength. Why should we seek to destroy one another when the whole world pushes to destroy us?"

"Sorcery," Ancion muttered.

Jilda rose. "Inca ruler, I witnessed the death of my predecessor at the hands of the Master Chiun. He used no sorcery. But if that is what you fear, then help me to stop this wicked contest."

"I fear no one! It is you who fear, because you are a woman, and by nature a coward."

Jilda's jaw clenched. She stared at the Inca for a long moment, as if fighting with herself. Then, exhaling suddenly, she pulled the dagger from her belt and leaped like a deer toward Ancion. He moved out of her way swiftly, pulling out his own knife.

It happened in a matter of seconds. Then, in another moment, a third pair of moving hands entered between then, snatched both daggers away, and thrust them upward, where they quivered embedded in the stone ceiling of the cave.

"This is why we have the tradition of the Master's Trial," Chiun said wearily, his hands still on their wrists. "This way, only four from each generation among us are destroyed."

Ancion jumped up and extricated his knife from the rock. He held it, hesitating as he watched the blank eyes of H'si T'ang. Then he slid the blade back into its sheath. "I will fight your apprentice. But if there is any trickery, my people will stand ready to tear his limbs and scatter his blood on the wind." He threw his cloak over his shoulder and left.

Chiun poured more tea into the remaining cups and cleared the Inca's things away. "Not the peaceful meeting I planned."

"It was my fault," Jilda said. "I attacked him." She hung her head. "I, who wished to abolish the bloodshed."

"Violence is a difficult habit to break among our kind," H'si T'ang said kindly. "It is the way of all our peoples. It is how we have survived."

"But we don't have to kill each other."

"That is for each of you to decide in your own heart." He turned to Emrys. "Tell me, will you resign from the contest?"

Emrys grunted. "I'll not be called a coward."

H'si T'ang nodded. "And you, Jilda. You would not permit yourself to be called a coward, either?"

"It is different for me. I'm a woman. I cannot be the only one to retreat. The elders of Lakluun would be shamed."

"I see. And you, Kiree? Would your elders be shamed?"

The little black man smiled. "Very much," he said. "You see, the Tellem do not believe in death. It is our belief that when we die, our spirits are transferred to others. That way, we continue to live. To fear shedding one life when there is promise of another at hand is most unworthy."

"We believe much the same thing here in Sinanju," H'si T'ang said.

Jilda sighed. "So the Master's Trial goes on. Because we are afraid to be afraid."

"That is so," H'si T'ang said.

They slept. The next morning, as the three warriors prepared to take their leave, Chiun gave each of them a polished piece of jade inscribed with Korean characters. "It is the symbl of the Master's Trial," Chiun said. "When my pupil comes to your lands for the contest, he will be carrying one of these so that you may recognize one another."

"What about Ancion?" Jilda asked.

Kiree laughed. "I think Ancion will have everyone in his country looking for the protegee of the Master of Sinanju."

Emrys strapped his knapsack onto his back. H'si T'ang moved toward him in the shadows. "Forgive me, but there is something about you, my son. Your aura. Something is wrong."

Emrys looked back quickly to Jilda and Kiree, standing in the doorway of the cave. "There's nothing wrong with me," he said loudly.

"It is your eyes—"

"My eyes are as good as anybody's. Good enough to fight your boy, at least," he bristled. Then he straightened up and smiled. "No offense, H'si T'ang. Whatever you did to Ancion's hands last night made a good show, but I don't cleave much to magic and hocus pocus myself. Besides, I can see just fine. Your aura locator made a mistake this time." He chuckled and joined the others at the door.

When they had left, Chiun turned to the old man and said, "The big one is becoming blind."

"I know. But he is too proud to admit it."

They settled near the fire. "And where is your successor now?" the old man asked.

"In America. But he will arrive here soon. I wish for you to meet him."

"Then his visit must be very soon, because my days are coming to an end," H'si T'ang said softly. "He is a good pupil?"

"Good enough," Chiun said, not wishing to boast about his protegee. "He is white."

"Oh?"

"But worthy," Chiun hastened to add. "That is, reasonably worthy. For a white."

H'si T'ang laughed. "I am making you uncomfortable," he said. "I do it out of amusement, because you are so painfully prejudiced."

"I did not wish to train a white boy. It just happened."

"It was meant to happen. Perhaps you do not know the legend. You are still so young."

Chiun was disconcerted. "I have lived more than eighty years, my teacher. No one would call me young."

H'si T'ang snorted. "Wait until you are my age. Even the mountains will appear young. You do know the legend, then?"

"Which legend? We have so many."

"The legend of Shiva." The old man spoke softly, remembering. "The ancient god of destruction will come to earth as a tiger wearing the skin of a man. He will be called the white night tiger, and he will die, to be created anew by the Master of Sinanju."

"I know the legend," Chiun said. "It has sustained me."

"And he is the one? The white night tiger?"

"I believe so. I have seen signs in him."

"And the boy? Does he know himself to be Shiva?"

Chiun shook his head. "He tries not to believe. Even when the signs exhibit themselves, he strives to forget. He is white, after all. What can one expect from a white thing?" He spat on the cave floor.

"He is only young. Too young, perhaps, to undertake the Master's Trial. He has not encountered opponents such as these contestants before, no doubt."

"No. Not like these."

"Take care of your godling, my son. This rite of passage is measured in blood."

Chiun stared at the fire for some time. "He is ready," he said at last.

H'si T'ang nodded. "Good," he said. "The scroll you took from my collection. Did you send it to him?"

"Yes, Little Father," Chiun said.

"Then you know the prophecy?"

"I do not understand it fully."

The old man smiled. His mouth was broad and toothless, and he grinned like a baby. "If the prophecies were perfectly understood, they would be history, not prophecy," he said, clapping Chiun on the back. "So. Tell me, son. What do you call your young, white, misplaced, nonbelieving pupil who bends his elbow during combat?"

Chiun looked up at him, startled. Then he smiled, because through the long years he had forgotten that his old teacher could still surprise him. "If you know he bends his elbow, then you know his name."

Chapter Two

His name was Remo and he was crawling into a whorehouse. That's all it was, Remo thought as he inched up the outside of the swank Fifth Avenue apartment house while a small colony of police waited impotently on the side-walk below. Only a whorehouse wasn't what you called any establishment in a building that rented space by the square inch.

It was an unlikely place for a group of sweat-stained terrorists, but then New York was a city that tolerated eccentricity, a term used to cover every type of pervert from the standard garden variety wand-waver to lunatics like the Managuan Liberation Front.

The MLF, as the group of unwashed, make-believe soldiers inside the whorehouse called itself, was a stock item in a city that specialized in mayhem: A handful of power-crazed fools who used international politics as an excuse to play with bombs. The MLF had tried to blow up four politically significant Manhattan buildings: the court-house, the prison known as the Tombs, and two police stations. But the bombs were so poorly made and the preparations so inadequate that they missed all four targets entirely and managed only to blast a lot of innocent by-standers to smithereens.

The one tactically intelligent thing the MLF crazies had thought up was to take refuge in the Versailles Arms. The tall, white marble building housed some of the richest people on the East Coast, and the MLF went to pains to select the richest and most celebrated among the tenants and hold them hostage in the discreet, thousand-dollar-a-night bordello on its top floor. Because of the danger to the hostages, the police were under orders not to storm the place in an all-out shoot-em-up, and were reduced to hanging around the entrances, waiting for the MLF to come out for air.

Remo didn't work for the police anymore. He was an employee of the United States government, but his name didn't appear on any federal payroll, since the nature of his work demanded a certain lack of publicity.

Remo was an assassin.

And an assassin, especially one as elaborately trained as Remo, could go places where no policeman would think of venturing. Like up the sheer face of a marble building.

When he reached the top story, his feet and hands using the momentum and weight of his body to scale the surface, he pushed away from the building and forced his legs upward into a backward spin that propelled him through a window in a shower of broken glass.

The room he vaulted into was, not surprisingly, a bedroom. The walls were covered with metallic mylar, and a chandelier hung from the center of the ceiling. On the oversized round bed were two swarthy young men wear-ing only purple berets marked by an insignia depicting a clenched fist with its middle finger outstretched. Standing over them was a leggy platinum blonde in a Nazi officer's cap satin garter belt, and thigh-high black leather boots with six-inch heels.

"Now they're coming in through the windows," she shrilled, throwing down the snakeskin whip in her hands. "I give up. First these twerps who haven't got two bits between the bunch of them, and now the human fly. I knew supply-side economics was leading to this. I suppose you're not going to pay, either."

Before Remo could answer, the two Managuans jumped out of bed, waving a pair of switchblades. On their hairless chests were tattoos bearing the words, "MLF" and "Free Managua."

"Hey, man, get your own poontang. The madam here's for us."

"Shut up, shitface," the blonde said. " 'Long as I'm giving it up for free, I choose him." She sidled up next to Remo. "At least he smells like he took a bath since last August."

She brushed a white-gold lock of hair out of her eyes. "Honestly," she grumbled. "These creeps are driving me crazy. They take over the building, they drive all my regular customers away. I've taken a net loss of thirty thousand bucks since they got here. And *kinky*. Let me tell you—"

"What you doing here, man?" one of the Managuans said, brandishing his knife. "This here's a revolution."

Remo glanced at his naked body, which looked as if it had been nurtured since infancy on a steady diet of tortilla chips and Coca Cola. "It's pretty revolting, all right," he agreed. "You're the terrorists, I guess."

"We're the *Front*, dude," the Managuans said, ribbing each other jocularly.

"Maybe you'd better switch to the back. The Front looks like it died."

"*You* gonna die, man." The switchblades moved closer.

"Look," Remo said. "I don't want to fight with you. I just washed my hands. How come you're doing this with the bombs and the hostages. . . ." He waved vaguely.

The man with "Free Managua" stenciled onto his chest fixed Remo with a practiced intense stare. "We're doing it 'cause we got political consciousness, baby." He pounded his tattoo. The gesture produced a jalepeño-scented belch. "We want independence from America. You strip our country, man. We ain't putting up with that."

"Aw, come on," Remo said. "There's nothing on Managua except hurricanes."

The Managuan looked uncertainly at Remo for a moment. "What else they done, Manuel?" he whispered out of the corner of his mouth.

Manuel thought hard, apparently expediting the process by probing his navel with his index finger. "I got it. We're sick of their honkey foreign aid."

The spokesman sprang to life again. "Right on. We don't need no stinking handouts. We want welfare."

"Wait a second," Remo said.

"Damn straight, man. Welfare's our right. We want to collect, just like the brothers here in New Jork." The two men saluted one another with upraised fists, their middle fingers extended proudly, and broke into a chant. "Free Managua! MLF! Power to the People! Boogie!"

"You know, I used to get a nice class of customer in here," the madam muttered.

The chant seemed to transport the Managuans into ecstasy. Manuel strutted up to Remo, slashing the air around Remo's face with his open blade and shouting, "Free our people. Like let my people go, dig it?" The two men slapped palms, twirling their knives high in the air while they performed the ritual.

Blankfaced, Remo stepped forward and picked the knives out of the air. He closed his fingers around them. For a moment there was a crackling sound. Then he opened his hands, and two mounds of metal filings sifted toward the floor. "Dig this," he said, and tossed the two men out the window.

"Hey, how'd you—" the blonde began, when she caught sight of a debonair gentleman standing in the bedroom's doorway. He was tall, with a refined nose and dark hair that was graying suavely at the temples. Remo recognized him as the conductor of an internationally famous symphony orchestra—a man who had been credited with promoting appreciation of classical music in America through his charm and sex appeal, although his tuxedo had been replaced by a transparent plastic shower curtain draped toga-style over one shoulder.

"What do you want now, Ray?" the madam asked irritably.

"I beg your pardon," the man said in pear-shaped tones. "My captors wish me to bring them a bottle of tequila. Could I put you to the trouble?"

"Tell those suckers to buy their own hooch, Maestro," the madam bellowed. "They're getting enough for free as it is."

"Oh, I assure you, I'll pay for the bottles myself."

"Hold it, hold it," Remo said. "You're one of the MLF's hostages, right?"

"Yes." The man showed a mouthful of dazzling white teeth. "I'm Raymond Rosner. Are you one of the liberators?" He extended his hand.

Remo slapped it away. "I don't shake hands with anybody who wears plastic before noon. Why are you buying tequila for them?"

"Well, they lead a very trying life," Rosner said earnestly. "It's the least I can do for these fine young men in their noble cause."

"What cause?"

"It's too complex to express in mere words."

"Try," Remo said.

The conductor blinked impatiently. "It is quite impossible for pampered capitalists such as ourselves to understand the inner rage of these valiant desperadoes. But I dig it. I absolutely dig it."

"Oh, I get it. You don't know what they want, either."

"Not really. Something about welfare. They abducted me from my apartment rather too hastily for us to enjoy a true rap session. But I'm sure they've got a good cause. I'm going to give a benefit performance for them after they release us."

"If they don't murder you first."

"We mustn't make generalizations about the lawlessness of the socio-economically repressed. Liberalism is more than just a word," Rosner said, winking. The wink changed into a mask of pain as a fat Managuan rushed in and kicked him in the kidneys, sending him sprawling face down on the floor.

"Where dat tequila?"

"Coming, bro," Rosner moaned.

The Managuan stepped on his neck. "I ain't your brother, honkey." He swaggered out into the corridor, toward a heavy metal door. Remo followed him.

"Right on," he heard Rosner croak from the bedroom carpet.

The door led to a steamy, white tiled chamber dominated by a giant hot tub filled with revelers. Aside from the fat Managuan and his cronies, plus several beautiful girls who Remo assumed worked for the establishment, there was a portly lady in her fifties, with yellow Shirley Temple curls and an impending case of turkey neck, a balding, pig-eyed little man, a nubile young girl whose chest displaced at least twenty gallons of water, and a skinny, seedy, middle-aged fellow with mercurochromecolored hair and a nose that seemed permanently engaged in the act of inhaling various drugs. There was something vaguely familiar about the man's distended nostrils.

"Hey, whoozat?" one of the Managuans asked, inclining a smoking joint toward Remo.

"I don't know, but he can come play in my bubble bath anytime," the fat lady squealed.

The young girl eyed Remo's physique and pronounced him "totally wow."

Remo looked around. The only member of the group of hostages and terrorists not immersed in the eight-foot round tub was a stringy, morose-looking man wrapped in a towel. He sat on a tile bench swigging periodically from a bottle of vodka.

"Bourgeois hedonists," the man growled in a thick Russian accent.

"Who're you?" Remo asked.

The man drank thoughtfully. "Who am I?" he mused. "What is 'I'? What is existence but the quintessential nothingness?"

"Forget it," Remo said. He walked over to a pile of dirty T-shirts and jeans. There was some grumbling from the hot tub as Remo scattered the clothes to reveal several shoddily constructed explosives and an Uzi submachine gun.

"Oh, great," he said, as he dismantled the bombs. He noticed a pair of long legs in boots standing next to him.

"I'm Francine," the madam purred.

"I recognized you." Remo's fingers moved swiftly.

"You're serious, aren't you?" she asked with some surprise. "About rescuing the hostages and my girls, I mean."

Remo expelled a gust of breath. "I'm supposed to rescue them. I don't have to take them seriously."

A smile spread across Francine's face. "You're cute. Maybe you want to party?"

"Can it, lady. I left my traveler's checks at home."

"I take American Express." She gestured toward the tub. "Now just look at those people. They're having a wonderful time. That little man's a millionaire builder, and that's his wife beside him, with the cocaine spoon. The groupie's with Freakie Dreems, the rock star. You've heard of him, haven't you?"

So that was why the nose looked familiar. It had become famous twenty years ago, in the "ugly is sexy" movement that Mr. Dreems had pioneered.

"Who's that?" Remo inclined his head toward the man with the vodka.

"Oh, that's Ivan Nyrghazy, the Russian novelist. He defected to America two years ago. He moved into this building after his book, *Nothing Is Everything* was made into a TV miniseries."

"Uh," Remo said as he unraveled the fuses of the bombs. He stood up. "I guess that takes care of the explosives, at least."

"What'd he do?" the fat Managuan said, rising out of the tub like a tattooed porpoise in gold bikini trunks.

"I defused your bombs, Baby New Year. They could have gone off any minute."

"I'll tell you what's going to go off, nosy." He grabbed the machine gun. "This."

Freakie Dreems clutched his forehead. "What *is* this drug?" he rhapsodized. "It's bending my mind. I just thought I saw someone pick up a machine gun."

"Gag me with a spoon," the groupie said abstractedly.

The Managuan fired. Bullets sprayed around the tiled enclosure like popcorn. Remo flung himself into a recess in the wall. The groupie leaped out of the tub, shimmying frantically as a cloud of white bubbles traveled spectacularly from her neck to her ankles.

Remo peeked out at the barrage of gunfire coming his way.

The Russian drank. "A moment of boredom, then nothingness," he intoned.

"I face bullets for this?" Remo muttered. But he couldn't afford to think about that now. Pulling himself up the tile wall quickly, he somersaulted away toward the gunner. He landed with his feet in the Managuan's soft abdomen. The machine gun flew into the air. Remo caught it and wrapped it like a scarf around the man's neck.

A second Managuan charged him. As he came forward, Remo studied the man's chest. Standing among the garish lettering of his tattoo were five lonely hairs. Remo used them as his focus. He thrust at the chest and tore off the man's tattoo, along with several layers of epidermis. The Managuan screamed.

"You pay for that, mother," another MLF representative said, pulling a knife from his beret and throwing it expertly toward Remo's throat. Remo stepped aside and waited for the blade to come within range. Then he flicked it with the end of his fingernail to send it boomeranging back to its owner.

The Managuan's face registered blank terror. He turned to run, but before he reached ninety degrees, the knife struck home, sliding through his temples with a swish. The Managuan stood still for a moment, then fell, the knife quivering in his forehead like a large silver fish.

"Grody to the max," the groupie said, chewing her gum energetically.

Francine wound her silken arms around Remo as the last two Managuans pulled themselves cautiously out of the hot tub and stalked over the tiles. "Violence excites me," she whispered, breathing heavily. "How about you?"

"It wears me out," Remo said, throwing off her embrace and darting forward to collar the two men. He picked them up, one in each hand, and propelled them against the tile wall near the tub. They landed with a splinter of bones, then slid noiselessly into the water, their corpses draping themselves over the hostages.

The fat lady and her husband screamed. Freakie Dreems stared hard at a glassine packet of pink powder.

"I don't care if it is two hundred simoleons a pop. I want some more," he said.

The Russian novelist waved his bottle over the throng. "Being . . . nothingness," he pronounced sagely.

Remo pulled the plug in the tub. "Okay, out." He prodded the hostages toward the entrance.

"Going so soon?" Francine asked, running her metallic-green fingernails through Remo's hair.

"I'm on my lunch hour."

She pouted. "You can't leave me like this. I've got to face all those police, and I'm probably going to get busted. So just a quickie for the road, okay?"

Remo sighed. Women were always doing this to him. "Will you settle for this?" he asked, pressing a small cluster of nerves on the inside of her left wrist.

Francine shivered. They always did. The left wrist was the beginning of a long series of steps that brought women to arousal. Remo had learned them as part of his training. Sometimes it was insulting, because most women preferred being touched on the wrist to making love. But then, nobody made love anymore. Pleasure seemed to be enough for women these days.

So Remo usually pleasured them for no reason other than to keep them peaceful. They didn't care about love, and neither did he. The mechanical execution of a pleasure formula, unfeeling, uncaring, unthinking, served everyone well.

When Francine began to moan, he switched to a place on her thigh, then progressed to an erogenous zone on her back. She shrieked and panted in ecstasy. He touched her neck, and she came screaming and writhing on the slippery floor.

Four steps. There were many more, but they usually weren't necessary. They certainly weren't for Francine.

"Well, that was fun," she said, brushing herself off.

The groupie was drooling. "To the max," she drawled reverently.

"Out. All of you. Get going." Remo herded them into the corridor.

"I must tell you that our rescue was quite satisfying," the Russian said as Remo lifted the still crumpled form of Raymond Rosner. "It was rather amusing, in fact. A speck of being in a sea of—"

"I know. Nothingness."

The Russian's eyebrows rose. "Very astute. I shall dedicate my next slim volume of verse, entitled 'Holes in the Fabric of Life' to you."

"Don't bother," Remo said. "I don't exist."

The novelist pondered. " 'I don't exist.' That's very profound. I don't exist."

Remo dumped the conductor into Ivan's arms. "Yeah, and I wish you didn't, either."

When the police stormed up the stairways and elevators, Remo left the way he had come. Down the building's side.

What he'd told the Russian had been true. There was no Remo Williams anymore. That man was dead, a young policeman executed in an electric chair for a crime he didn't commit. Ah, justice, he thought. Raymond Rosner was going to raise money so that the Managuan Liberation Front could make more bombs, but a rookie cop with some faked evidence against him gets fried in the chair.

The chair hadn't worked. It was planned from the beginning that the young policeman wouldn't die. He was only to appear to have died so that his name and face and fingerprints and files were taken permanently off everyone's records.

Remo's identity had been so effectively erased so that he could serve a new agency of the United States government. No one except the president and the director of the organization were to know about it, or Remo. The agency was called CURE, and it was illegal in every sense of the word. CURE operated outside the Constitution to fight crime with the ultimate means: an assassin.

Remo had not wanted to be the enforcer arm of a secret, illegal government organization, but once he had been declared dead, there were few options left to him. At first, Remo had felt as if he were living in a nightmare: the frame, prison, the chair. . . . And then the endless days at Folcroft Sanitarium, a quiet nursing home in Rye, New York, run by a mild-mannered, unimaginative, middle-aged man named Dr. Harold W. Smith, who was the director of CURE. Smith hired a teacher to undertake the task of Remo's training, and the nightmare became worse.

The teacher was a crazy old Korean named Chiun, who seemed to feel that an ordinary man could be taught to achieve the physically impossible. Remo would have written Chiun off as just another strange element in the weird circumstances that surrounded him, except that the old Oriental could himself perform all the outlandish tasks he assigned to Remo.

Chiun could walk with such lightness that he did not even break the membranes of dried leaves that lay under his feet. He could move so swiftly that he could not be seen, and so silently that he could not be heard. He could hear the ultrasonic calling of insects. He could see the pollen on a butterfly's wings in flight. And he could kill more effectively than anyone on earth.

Chiun was from a village named Sinanju in a remote area of North Korea, where the martial art had been born and had been evolving for thousands of years. But the teachings of Sinanju went further than the acquisition of physical strength. It was the sun source of the martial arts, the original from which the pale imitations of jujitsu, karate, aikido, t'ai chi chu'an, and tae kwon do sprang. As such, the followers of Sinanju learned to develop their senses and minds to an uncanny degree as well. It was for this reason that the Masters of Sinanju had been in demand as assassins in wealthy, distant lands since the time of the first Master Wang more than a millennium ago.

The training was a long and difficult process. Only one man of Sinanju at a time was groomed to be Master, and he spent his entire life in learning and practice. When it was time, the Master trained a new pupil to take his place.

Chiun had trained his own apprentice, Nuihc, to manhood. But something went wrong. At the time when the Master's pupil should have been preparing himself for a life of service to his village, Nuihc turned on Chiun and held Sinanju in terror. He was stopped, but not without great sacrifice to Chiun. At Nuihc's death, Chiun, who was already an old man, was left without an heir. There would be no Masters of Sinanju after him.

Then, called into service for Harold Smith and CURE, he found an answer in the white boy named Remo. It was not a suitable answer, since Remo was not even from the village, but he showed some promise.

He worked with Remo and changed him from a beefy ex- G.I. who wasn't bad in a fistfight to a thin, finely tuned instrument of death. In those years Remo had also become, spiritually and emotionally, Chiun's son. The rare and magnificent tradition of the Masters of Sinanju had been passed down to him. He was now a Master and would someday be *the* Master.

And he was using it all to rout a bunch of gun-happy adolescents from a bordello. Old Wang was surely turning over in his urn, Remo thought as he recalled the events of the day.

The Managuans weren't an assignment. They were an embarrassment. Not to mention the people he'd stuck his neck out to save. Anybody who used phrases like "quintessential nothingness" deserved to drown in a hot tub.

Things weren't supposed to turn out this way. Chiun didn't spend the best years of his life watching interpretive dances to machine gun fire. Where was the challenge of the traditions of Sinanju for Remo?

He had left Manhattan and was striding along a river-bank leading upstate. Instead of bringing him serenity, the clean, still air of the countryside made the burdens of his emotions even heavier. It occurred to him that perhaps he had just been born too late. Maybe the glory of Sinanju was just a legend now, relegated to the distant past where legends thrive. The modern world, Remo's world, had no place for heroes.

Yet there had once been a man who had taxed all of Remo's resources. A strange, terrible man who could fight every bit as well as Remo.

No, he thought angrily. Keep the record straight. The Dutchman had fought better than Remo.

Because he not only understood the subtle discipline of Sinanju as well as Remo did, but he was also equipped with a mutant mind so advanced and unique that it con-trolled whatever it fixed on. The Dutchman had frightened Remo. It was a sensation he missed. In a life filled with losers like the Managuan Liberation Front, the sheer skill of an opponent as horrifying as the Dutchman was worthy of respect.

But the Dutchman was long dead. Not by Remo's hand;

he hadn't been able to do it. Even now, the knowledge that the Dutchman's death had occurred through forces of nature and not Remo's ability still galled him. It had been his one chance to test himself to the limit, and he hadn't been up to the job. And never, he knew, never would it come again.

The Folcroft Sanitarium complex came into view. "Oh, what difference does it make, anyway?" Remo said aloud. He wasn't some freelance hero searching for adventure at the bidding of the gods, after all. He was just a guy with a job, and for that job he had been trained more expertly than anyone else on earth. It was useless to spend his time moping about inadequate adversaries, because Remo and Chiun were, since the Dutchman's death, the only people alive who even knew anything about Sinanju. Besides, he reasoned, it wasn't as if he didn't have anything to do. Challenge or no challenge, there were enough murderous yo-yos around to keep him busy for the next 600 years.

Just drop it, he told himself. He'd take off for a while, to someplace beautiful and sunny where the girls showed a lot of skin, and he'd be as good as new. He climbed the steps leading to Folcroft's main double doors. Tahiti. That was where he was going. Tahiti was perfect. Chiun would like it, too. The old man liked coconuts.

Mrs. Mikulka, Smith's secretary, made the usual fuss about her boss's instructions to be left undisturbed, and as usual, Remo beat her to the door and let himself in. Smith was squinting hard at a piece of paper in his hand and reciting from it, a look of extreme discomfort permeating his lemony features.

"On wings of dust gather we into the Void. . . . Good God." He turned when Remo entered. "Oh, it's you," he said irritably.

"Thank you for the usual warm reception, Smitty.

Where's Chiun? I figured the sub from Sinanju ought to be back by now."

"That is correct," Smith said tersely. "The submarine has returned. Chiun, however, was not aboard."

Remo was alarmed. "Is he—"

"He is not spiritually disposed to return at the moment. At least that's what he told the captain. He sent along an Ung poem instead." He waved the paper at Remo.

"The Song of the Butterfly," Remo read. "Oh, that's a good one. Wang's finest. Catchy verse."

"Remo, I dispatched a Navy submarine to venture quite illegally into enemy waters just for the purpose of picking Chiun up from his holiday. The captain is extremely distressed, to say the very least."

"Nothing else? Didn't he send any message for me?"

"Yes, yes," Smith said crankily. He picked up a scroll tied with a reed ribbon and handed it to Remo. "This is for you."

Remo unrolled the aged parchment and read the fading Korean characters.

He is created Shiva, the Destroyer; death; the shatterer of worlds; the dead night tiger made whole by the Master of Sinanju.

Below were another set of characters:

The Master will die by the hand of the Other in the spring of the Year of the Tiger. And the Other will join with his own kind. Yin and yang will be one in the Year of the Tiger.

The parchment, finally exposed to light and humidity after centuries of storage, cracked and disintegrated in his hands.

"Aw, come on," Remo said.

"What is it?"

"A story," Remo thought about it. "A dumb story."

"What does he want?"

"I think he wants me to go to Sinanju."

"Well, you can't go on a United States submarine," Smith said.

"I'm not going at all. I've waited for this vacation, and I'll be damned if I'm going to spend it in North Korea."

Smith gave a small shrug and leafed through some computer printouts on his desk. He checked his watch. "Er . . . your vacation has begun. Report back to me in ten working days."

Remo dusted the shards of parchment off his knees and swept out of the building.

He'd had it. This time he'd really had it with the old man's sneaky methods of luring him to Sinanju. The place was a pit. And he really needed a healthy dose of Tahiti. Now Chiun would gripe and complain for the next six months about Remo's not showing up when he was summoned by some melodramatic chicken scratches.

For dinner, he ate some rice in a third-rate Chinese restaurant, then went back to his motel room and turned on the television. Chiun can take his vacation by himself for once, he told himself. There's no reason why Remo had to spend two weeks in misery just to keep the old man company. He turned the volume on the television higher.

Still, what did it mean? The Shiva nonsense at the beginning was for him, he was sure of that. Chiun took some kind of perverted satisfaction in pretending that Remo was the reincarnation of some Indian spirit with a dozen arms. For the life of him, Remo could never figure out why. But the rest of it. The Master will die. . . . Which Master? Wang? The scroll had obviously been written centuries ago.

And who—or what—was the Other?

He turned the sound on the television up to ear-shattering level. The legends and traditions of Sinanju irked Remo to no end. In the first place, he couldn't understand them. And in the second place, he'd just received a day-long demonstration of how little the mystique of Sinanju affected his daily life.

Dross. It was all just a bunch of baloney to further complicate Remo's already complicated existence. The legends had as much relevance to Remo as the man in the moon.

But Chiun was old. He lived in the past. Let it go. He went over to the television again, found it wouldn't go any louder, and sat back down.

When was the Year of the Tiger? He tried to remember the calendar system used by the ancient Masters of Sinanju. The Tiger was a wild and ferocious beast, beautiful and deadly, swift and quiet and unpredictable. The year would be a time of changes and reversals, unexpected challenges, sudden surprises. It was . . . He counted on his fingers.

Then, feeling his heart thudding in his chest, he got up and turned off the television. He sprinted out the door and headed back to Folcroft. Chiun hadn't written the message. The scroll had belonged to the collection among the ancient archives. And yet it had been a warning. Or a cry for help. Which Master—Chiun or Remo? One of them was going to die at the hands of someone—Male? Female? Machine? Spirit?—called "the Other."

And it was going to happen soon, because this was May. It was the spring of the Year of the Tiger.

Chapter Three

Remo arrived soaking wet upon the shores of Sinanju.

"Tell Smitty I love him, too," he mumbled after the rapidly submerging submarine in the distance. Leave it to Smith to stipulate that the sub deposit Remo a mile from shore.

Well, at least he'd arrived. Smith's loud protests notwithstanding, Remo managed to wrangle a ride to the place for which, now that he was actually seeing it, the term "pit" seemed woefully inadequate.

Sinanju was cold and rocky. Its shores, lapped by menacing, steel gray waves, looked like the backdrop in a Frankenstein movie. The only visible forms of life were the lichens and barnacles that grew on the jagged boulders in the sea. But there were other life forms here, Remo reminded himself as he stepped gingerly toward the village.

Snakes. Sinanju was literally crawling with snakes, most of them poisonous. If there was one thing memorable about this wasteland so desolate that even Chairman Mao hadn't bothered to send propaganda here, it was the snakes. Remo lifted his foot in the tall grass to allow one to slither

by. A brief thought of the dream that was Tahiti flickered
in his mind and died there. Remo shrugged. Tahiti would
be around for the next vacation, whenever that would be.
Chiun needed him now.

An old man walking along the shore a hundred yards
away signaled him with a rough-hewn cane. Remo met
him. "You wanted to speak to me?" he asked politely in
Korean. He noticed that the old man was blind.

"Your teacher awaits you. I will take you to him."

Remo looked around, confused. There was no one else
in sight. "Are you sure you have the right person?"

"You are Remo, are you not? The Master Chiun waits
within a cave not far from here."

"How—how did you know I was coming today?"

The old man smiled. "I knew. My name is H'si T'ang."

"Chiun's teacher? But I thought . . ." Remo caught
himself.

"I was dead? No, I am not dead yet. In Sinanju, when a
Master lives to pass on his title to his successor, he is
obliged to enter a period of seclusion for many years.
During that time, the new Master is not permitted to speak
of his mentor, for the retired Master must be left in
absolute peace. But now my time of seclusion is past."

He led Remo deftly through the ragged high grass,
pointing out moving snakes with his walking stick. "There
is a colony of vipers to your left," he said, walking briskly
past a deep, sandy pit alive with slithering forms. "Very
dangerous. At rest, their long fangs rest horizontally in
their mouths, but when they are enraged, the poison ar-
rows spring into view. It is a most alarming sight."

Remo looked down at the pit, then at the old man's
milky white eyes. "Can you see them?" he asked.

"Not as you see," he said warmly. "But remember, we
are in Sinanju. Your eyes are but one tool of many in your

possession. You must be prepared to use all your tools, all your knowledge here. The cave lies ahead."

Remo liked the old man. There was a strange aura about him, a field of crystalline intensity that seemed to emanate from him, that Remo found pleasant. The cave they were walking toward exuded the same feeling.

"Nice flowers," he said, noticing the spare, beautiful arrangement of plants outside the cave's entrance.

"Those are my friends," the old man said, his face crinkling happily. "They remind me of a poem written by Yun Son Do in the seventeenth century. It is called 'The Five Friends.' " He recited:

> How many friends have I? Count them:
> Water and stone, pine and bamboo—
> The rising moon on the east mountain,
> Welcome, it too is my friend.
> What need is there, I say,
> To have more friends than five?

Remo smiled. "Well, it's better than Ung poetry."

"So is the sound of a donkey braying. I detest the Ung," H'si T'ang said. "It is a form which appeals only to old-fashioned purists."

"Chiun likes Ung poetry."

"I know. I have been forced to listen to it all these weeks." He gestured with his head toward Chiun, who was sitting in lotus position on the fragrant grass mat in the cave, scribbling furiously with a feather on a parchment scroll. "There will be more Ung tonight, I'm afraid," he whispered.

Remo stared at the slight figure bent over the parchment. "I thought you were sick," he said.

"That is typical," Chiun answered. "I send you a clear message about participating in the Master's Trial, and you interpret it as a sign of disease. H'si T'ang, this is the oafish white thing on which I have wasted the knowledge of Sinanju.'' He went back to his work.

"Remo and I have met," the old man said, pinching Remo's arm affectionately. "I will prepare tea."

When he had gone, Remo went over to Chiun and snatched the quill out of his hand. "Do you mean to tell me that you're perfectly all right?"

"Of course I'm all right." He grabbed the quill back. A dollop of ink splashed onto the parchment. "Look what you have caused now!" he shrieked. "It is ruined! The most sublime piece of Ung since the Great Wang himself."

"Forget Ung. I gave up my whole vacation to come here because I thought you needed me. I think I deserve an explanation."

"All was explained in my missive," Chiun said loftily.

"All that scroll said was some craziness about yin and yang and somebody called the Other, who was going to kill the Master. I'd like to know what that was about, if you don't mind."

H'si T'ang entered with the tea. "Yin and yang, my son, are the two halves of a whole," he said. "Light and darkness, good and evil, life and death. One must always balance the other. It is the way of all being."

Remo stared at him. "Uh, sure," he said. What the hell, he thought. Old people were allowed to be a little nuts.

Chiun looked up from his writing. "There was no mention of the Master's Trial?"

"The what?"

Chiun placed a finger to his lips, thinking. "Perhaps I forgot to include the note about the Master's Trial," he said. "Well, no matter. You are here now."

"For *what*?" Remo shouted.

"Lower your voice in this place."

"He has a right to be angry," H'si T'ang said. "He

does not yet understand his purpose here." He handed a cup to Remo. "We shall explain, my son."

They told him about the rules of the Master's Trial and the names of the opponents he was to face in combat.

"Do you have any questions?"

Remo opened his mouth to speak, but no words came out. He tried again. "You've got to be kidding," he said.

"I assure you, o silver-tongued orator, this is not a joke," Chiun said tightly. "It is one of the oldest traditions of Sinanju."

Remo leaned forward. "Let me get this straight. You want me to go around the world, without any money or even any food in my pockets, and fight a bunch of characters I've never even met?"

"That is correct." Both old men were smiling serenely.

"Well, I hate to break it to you, but that's the wackiest idea I ever heard. No thanks."

"Listen to how the young reject the sacred ways of the old," Chiun screeched. "I am ashamed, o Master, woefully ashamed of the pale piece of pig's ear I was deceived into training as my pupil. For this, I deserve to enter into the Great Void before my time. For this—"

"Calm yourself," H'si T'ang said, patting Chiun's knee. He turned to Remo. "But why, my son, do you refuse?"

Remo sputtered. "Because it's a crazy idea. I don't have anything against Jildo the Viking, or whoever he is. Why should I kill him?"

"It is not understood that you will kill anyone. Perhaps they will kill you."

"Come on. A bunch of half-naked aborigines who've been living in the past for a thousand years? I don't have to prove anything by slaughtering them."

"The Master's Trial is a necessary rite of passage for all Masters of Sinanju. No emperor would hire an assassin who has not completed his training," Chiun said.

"I'm already working."

"Only for the United States," Chiun sniffed. "There are other governments."

"I'm satisfied with one."

Chiun got up and walked out. "Lout," Remo heard him mutter at the entrance to the cave.

Remo and H'si T'ang sat in silence. The old man poured more tea with exquisite grace. Finally he said, "Do you know the legends of Shiva the Destroyer, my son?"

Remo sighed. "I've heard them. And heard them. And heard them."

"But you do not believe that you are his reincarnation."

"I'm Remo Williams. I used to be a cop in Newark, New Jersey. All I know is, if I was a god who wanted to come to earth, Newark isn't the place I'd pick. I think Chiun's imagination went overboard on that one."

H'si T'ang nodded. "And the Master's Trial is an unnecessary annoyance for you."

"I just don't see why I have to murder a bunch of total strangers."

"I see. You feel that the other participants pose no challenge to you?"

"Well, I don't want to seem conceited, but—"

With a motion so swift that Remo never saw it coming, the old man pinned him to the floor by his neck, pressing on nerves that made it impossible for Remo to move his arms and legs. Remo stared up, terrified, at the sightless eyes. Then, as quickly as he had attacked, H'si T'ang released Remo and helped him up.

"Forgive me, but I felt it necessary to demonstrate my point. You see, I too, looked with disdain upon the ancient peoples until I met with them during my Master's Trial."

Remo rubbed the place on his neck where the old man's hands had gripped it. "So? You won."

"Not without great difficulty. Not one of your opponents would have missed my attack."

Remo looked at the floor.

"These are not primitive humans. They are highly advanced in their ways, and are to be respected. You will see that for yourself if you go. But if you continue to refuse, the warriors of these lands will be greatly insulted, and will make war on us. They will destroy the village as a point of honor."

"You mean they'll kill me if I don't fight them?"

"Perhaps not you, but all the innocent people of Sinanju who have relied for so many centuries on the Master to protect them. They themselves have never learned how to fight." The old man took his hand. "Chiun is still too young and proud to beg, even for his people. But I am not. Remo—"

"Don't," Remo said. "I'll go. I didn't understand."

"The Ritual of Parting will be tomorrow," H'si T'ang said.

By the light of dawn, the two Masters led Remo from the cave to a small wooden boat bobbing near the shore. Chiun was dressed in a red silk kimono with a small black hat that looked like a series of boxes stacked on his head. For the procession, he carried a strange-looking musical instrument with sixteen bronze bells, which he struck with a wooden mallet. The music it made was supposed to be the essence of peace and beauty, but Remo thought it sounded like loose change clinking in a pocket. H'si T'ang dressed in black. On his head he wore the high, spiky crown of gold that the Masters of Sinanju had worn since the Middle Ages.

Chiun gave Remo a polished jade inscribed with three Korean characters. "Your opponents all have similar stones, except for Ancion," he said. "They will find you through it."

Remo read the characters. "The Brotherhood," he read. "I thought these guys were supposed to be my enemies."

"Perhaps you will learn something of enmity and friendship on this journey," Chiun said as Remo got into the boat.

"There's just one thing before I go. In the scroll you sent me, it said something—"

"The Other," H'si T'ang said. He sniffed the ocean air. "He is coming. Beware."

Chiun looked at H'si T'ang. "Who is he, my teacher?"

"I cannot see. But someone close, very close. His spirit is near. We are deceived. The Other is of two beings. Yin and yang . . ." His words drifted off, and H'si T'ang shook his head rapidly. "The vision is gone."

"The Other," Remo mused. "A fifth opponent?"

"I do not know who he is, only that he comes."

"For me?" Remo asked.

"He is coming for us all." With a quick swat of his right hand, the old man's long fingernails sliced through the rope that bound the boat to shore, and Remo drifted out to sea. The last thing he heard was the music of Chiun's ancient instrument, and this time it sounded sad and forlorn.

Chapter Four

Two weeks had gone by and he couldn't reach Remo.

For the first time in all his years running the organization, Harold W. Smith felt his sparse breakfast come up in his throat. A nightmare. But worse.

With a nightmare, Smith would have awakened next to his wife of more than thirty years, Irma, and then gone back to sleep.

With a nightmare, he would sleep it off, then come to the office in the morning, say good morning to his secretary, who believed that he was Dr. Harold W. Smith, head of Folcroft Sanitarium, and then he would quietly close the soundproof, rayproof doors of his office overlooking Long Island Sound in Rye, New York, and get about his real business.

He would boot up that special bank of four computers from which he watched the inner workings of the world through a vast network that did not know exactly who it was working for.

Then if he saw special trouble, he would dial his special numbers and reach Remo and send him in. That was reality, the way his life worked, and that was the way the morning had begun, with the world working the way it should, and the lemony-faced man in the three-piece gray suit observing the bowels of the world, ready to do for his nation what it could not legally do itself.

That was his mission, and he had served it all his life, from the early days in the OSS, and then to the CIA, and then keeping his promise to Irma, staying home. She did not know he was also keeping his promise to a long-dead president that he would not let America be overthrown by its enemies. He ran the secret agency CURE, and no one knew save Smith, the president, Remo and Chiun. No one else, because to know was to die.

In the days before computers were common, CURE had them. And when others had them, CURE had models that outstripped them. Through the computers, the Folcroft Four, Smith could jump any message sent anywhere and have it captured, analyzed, and reported to him in minutes.

He had served his country for more than forty years, and he had never thought he would see the awesome power of his farflung network looking back at him through a monitor screen, telling him he was helpless. But that was the reality of the nightmare he was now living.

It had been a normal day on the screen, starting out with a report of the most recent events, and then moving on to analyze the primary dangers. This day, on the screen, there appeared a new method of importing cocaine into America. Instead of small shipments by plane or briefcase, it was now massive shipments to a point in Los Angeles. He dismissed that. The narcotics bureau could handle that, probably with the Coast Guard's help.

Smith moved on.

A judge in Minneapolis was taking bribes. A job for the FBI. He moved on.

A cabinet member in a crucial decision-making position

was investing in certain defense industries, using his insider's knowledge. Smith thought about that for a moment, then moved on. The Internal Revenue Service would get the cabinet member, either soon or later.

And then another message. A plot to kill the president of the United States.

He was about to direct the computer to slip that information into the hands of the Secret Service when he was caught short by a curious reference contained in the message.

"Group here confident 'B' will arrange intro. B assures target will be available. B assures Secret Service no problem. B as close to target as his pompadour. Target assured."

Harold Smith froze the message on the screen. The people planning to kill the president had an inside person. Someone was going to set up the president of the United States to be murdered, and it was going to be an inside job.

Quickly, he tried to scan from other sources whether the Secret Service had picked this up.

They hadn't. The hit group was somewhere in Virginia and waiting for word. The word was 1 P.M. Smith looked at his watch.

It was 12:30 P.M.

He forced the computers to bust into the Secret Service system and made sure the message was intercepted.

It was 12:40 when the secreen blinked. The Secret Service had picked up the message that Smith had fed into their computers. And there was a new message from the Folcroft computers. In twenty minutes, at 1 P.M., the president of the United States would be dead.

Smith opened a combination lock on a left desk drawer. Inside was a red phone. He stared at it. He could reach the president on that, and the president could reach him.

But what could he tell him that the Secret Service couldn't?

His computers reported at 12:45, that the Secret Service had not yet notified the president. What were they waiting for?

At 12:50, he used his computers to jump into the Secret Service system with an order to tell the president that someone close to him was going to kill him. The order would appear in the Secret Service computer system as if it came from an Undersecretary of Defense.

At 12:55, the president had still not been notified that he was going to be killed, and Harold W. Smith picked up the red telephone. It had no dial, but it needed none. It guaranteed instant access, because an identical telephone was always with the president, wherever he was.

Smith heard the gentle hum through the red receiver. It was 12:58 p.m. The president was not on the line. Smith, might have waited too long.

It was 12:59. The receiver was still humming. Smith's breakfast came up into his mouth with acid. The receiver sweated in his hands. His own secretary, who thought he really ran a sanitarium, was buzzing him about some doctor's meeting. He punched back into a keyboard which assistant should handle it.

Ten seconds more. It was nearing 1 P.M. and the phone clicked and the voice came on. Damn it, it was cheery. How could that man be so cheerful? This was the first time this president had used the red phone.

"Well, hello," came the pleasant voice as if he were glad to be on the phone so suddenly. "What can I do for you?"

"Sir," said Smith, but before he could speak, he heard the explosion. It sounded like a massive tidal wave smashing against a cliff. He winced instinctively, moving the telephone from his ear for a split second.

"Hold on," the president said. "Someone's been hurt."

Through the telephone, Smith could hear the hysterics.

Secret Service men were all around now. A doctor had been called in. Smith was not even sure what room the red phone had been answered in. He thought it might have been the private dining room because someone was talking about the plates being destroyed. Someone picked up the phone. It was a woman's voice.

"Hello, who is this?" she asked. "Who is this?"

Smith did not answer. He would speak only to the president.

"Who is this? You're being very rude. Do you know how rude? Someone has just tried to kill the president."

The woman hung up.

He could not have talked to her. He could use that telephone only to speak to the president, and now, why bother? The attempt to kill him had already been made.

Someone had almost killed the president. Something was wrong with the Secret Service protection, and the White House had had some sort of enemy agent inside it. Only one thing could save the president now. To wrap the most effective pair of killing hands and eyes into the White House, to stay at the president's side, until the killers tried again.

Smith reached out for his killer arm. And then the nightmare began. The two weeks of authorized vacation for Remo was over but he couldn't reach him. He tried him on a primary number and then on a secondary number. Finally he tried one more number, just on a chance. It was a number set up by Chiun, for what purposes Smith could never understand. The phone rang three times. No answer. A fourth ring. And then an answer. A recorded message.

Chiun's voice.

"Hello. Be heartened that you have not reached a wrong number. The number is totally correct. It is you who are incorrect. But if you are not totally incorrect and you call to render homage to a person far better than any other you have known, then record your message briefly at the signal. I may well get back to you. I have gotten back to other people before.''

Beeeeep.

"Chiun, this is Smith. I have to talk to you immediately. Contact me right away.''

Smith held the phone, hoping that Chiun would come on, but the receiver went dead.

Where are they? Smith wondered. He had to reach Remo. Even Chiun would do in a pinch, although Chiun never quite understood what CURE's mission was, and Smith had trouble dealing with the aged Oriental who had taken Remo and made him into an assassin unlike anything ever imagined in the western world before.

The computer monitor was reporting again.

The operatives in Virginia were notifying their home base again. Smith sent his computers into a tracking mode but he could not pick up who these operatives worked for. They were transmitting in code, which Folcroft's computers easily broke, but every time his computer analyzed source and emission to track the would-be killers, frequencies were changed, and he was unable to pin down the killers' location.

Now something else was happening. Instructions were being given.

"So much for B's assurance about a 1 P.M. completion. B move when? Must be day. Give time.''

"Six A.M. The White House,'' came the response.

"B assures?''

"B assures,'' the other party to the dialogue responded.

Whoever was arranging the killing of the president was code-named B. He was somewhere in Virginia. Smith knew that, but he could find nothing else, and he realized he was sitting, staring at his monitor, helpless, watching his president go to his death. And he could not reach Remo.

For the first time in his adult life, he wished he could literally not know something. His stomach twisted. Breathing was hard. He realized one could not be involved in a life-and-death situation, while being seated, without the body doing strange things. The body, at this time, was meant to move. It could not take all that tension and adrenalin while sitting.

He glanced out through the windows of his office. Summer would soon be in the land. It would be beautiful, but he was helpless.

And then there was a call on his other private line. Remo's access line.

Smith had gotten through and he felt relieved. He would not have to tell the president about the danger without also telling him that the man who would protect him from that danger would be on his way to make sure the president was alive for breakfast.

"Yes," said Smith, the electricity of joy coursing through his body while his face, in its stiff Yankee rectitude, showed nothing. An observer would have thought the man was a bank vice-president making a decision on the lunch hours of different tellers.

"Oh, Gracious Emperor." The voice was not Remo's. It was Chiun.

"Chiun, I've got to get Remo immediately," Smith said.

"And you will. He will be at your devoted service to the glory of your name and through the everlasting reign of your graciousness."

"When?"

"When the slightest command issues from your imperial lips, o, Emperor, the House of Sinanju stands like a beacon of glory behind the infinite majesty of your command.''

''I would like to speak to Remo now,'' said Smith. He was uncomfortable with being called ''Emperor.'' The House of Sinanju had been assassins to monarchs of the world since before Rome was founded, but until Chiun no master had ever worked for a secret organization. Remo explained to Smith one day that Chiun could not understand anyone killing for any reason but to increase one's power. Chiun fully expected Smith, any day, to make some intricate and devious move to become president himself, and Chiun had promised that he would be there to stand at Smith's side when he proclaimed himself emperor. In anticipation of that day, he had already given Smith the title.

''Whatever is your wish, Emperor,'' Chiun said.

''I'll hold on. I want to talk to Remo now.''

''An emperor should never wait for his assassin. The assassin should wait for his emperor. Glory to you,'' came the squeaky voice. ''We stand ready to hang your enemies' heads by the walls of your city.''

''Where is Remo?''

''Serving you through glorifying the name of the House of Sinanju.''

''I have to talk to him now.''

''I would never be one to say no to an emperor,'' Chiun said.

''Where are you calling from?'' Smith asked.

''I am in Sinanju. This is the only telephone,'' Chiun answered proudly.

''And where is Remo?''

''He is at work.''

''What specifically is he doing that he cannot come to the phone now? I've got to have a specific answer, Chiun. Specific.''

Smith listened, nodding every now and then. Chiun talked for 3.5 minutes. The computer had that. The computer also recorded what Chiun had said so Smith could go over it again. The computer could put the old Korean's sing-song English into print and also analyze most probable meanings. When Chiun was finished talking and Smith was finished questioning, he turned to the computer to try to understand what he had heard.

The computer struggled and then quantified. There was a 98.7 percent certainty that Remo was off somewhere at some form of contest and could not be bothered with saving the life of just another American president. There was a 38.6 percent possibility that this contest had something to do with his training.

The computer had understood nothing else.

It was 4 P.M. when Harold W. Smith used the red telephone again. He waited, his face impassive. He did not have Remo, but it was not a time to dwell on what one did not have. One did with what one had, no matter how deficient. He had learned that as a child growing up in the small New Hampshire town. You did not boast. You did not shirk. You did not complain. You made do.

Somehow he remembered Irma while waiting for his president to answer. She was so pretty then. She was the rich girl of the town, and he thought he would die when he had to wear patched trousers to school, because he knew his desk would be near hers. But he went. It was as hard then to wear those trousers to the school as it was now to tell his president about an attempt on his life and that he had no means of protecting the president. He was going to have to tell his president he had failed.

"Hello again," came the friendly voice. "We had a bit of a to-do here. You know a bomb went off right here in the White House. If I hadn't gone to take your phone call, it would have gotten me."

"There is going to be another attempt on your life at 6 A.M. tomorrow."

"They'd better not succeed. I don't have time to die."

"Sir, not only has your protective shield been penetrated, but your Secret Service somehow doesn't seem able to respond."

"Well, then, I guess it's your job. You can do it. The president before me said that the only regret he had was that he didn't use your people on the Iranian hostage thing. You take care of it and let me get back to work. I work until five."

"Mr. President, that specific enforcement arm that your predecessor spoke of is engaged elsewhere."

"I see," the president's voice said mellowly over the phone. "Well, if it's more important than my life, I accept that. I'll try to work things out here. The Secret Service has been compromised, you say?"

"I'm not sure, sir. It could be some glitch in their communications. Very easily could be that."

"I see. Well, if I have to die, I won't be the first American to do it in the line of duty. But as your president, I would like to know what I'm dying for. I'd like to know what your people are involved in, what's more important to the country than the shock of losing another president in office."

Smith looked at the phone. The two worst fears of his professional life, a long life in service to his country, had just arrived at the earpiece of the special red phone: having to tell the president he had failed and having to give a stupid answer. His mouth tasted of bitter soda water.

"Sir, as near as I can make out, the enforcement arm you speak of is engaged in something that has to . . ."

"Yes?" the president said. "I'm really interested."

"We'll have someone into the White House with you by late tonight, sir. A somewhat older man," Smith said.

"Oh, the Oriental. Golly, I've heard of him. Over eighty, I was told, but I don't every have to worry about growing old, not once I see him in action. How old is he exactly?"

"The one we'll be sending is in his sixties and is Caucasian. He has what has been described as a lemony face and speaks with a New England accent."

"If you fellows have some age cure, let me know about it," the president said, chuckling.

"No sir, we don't," Smith said. The president was taking with good grace the fact that an old administrator who had not fired a planned shot for more than thirty years was now the only one standing between him and his death.

Harold W. Smith shut down the computer access codes from his office in Folcroft, reducing to only one portable device the ways to reach his computers. The device fit into his briefcase.

Gun, he thought. *Now where did I put the gun?*

Then he realized his gun wasn't in his office. It was home.

He told his office secretary, who thought he spent too much time cooped up in his office, that he would be gone for a few days, possibly a few weeks. He authorized her to make any decisions that had to be made and to sign any papers that needed signatures.

A few days, possibly a few weeks. He did not tell her possibly even a bit longer than that. Like forever. If he did not contact his computers within any 168-hour period, automatically the entire network would erase itself and no evidence would be left that the organization ever existed. Remo and Chiun, of course, would be on their own.

Something had gone wrong, but it had been going wrong for many years. It was only when Smith was in his house, holding his old pistol in his hands, that he realized fully what had happened over the years. You didn't see change when it was gradual; and sometimes it took many years to see motive.

Remo had been recruited in his special way because he was an American patriot. Now he had become something else. The enforcement arm was off somewhere enforcing something else.

Chiun had trained more than Remo's body; he had trained his soul. The whole organization came down to a window on the world through which everything could be seen, but nothing could be done, and now its strongest enforcement arm was an old gray-haired man searching through an old bureau drawer for a 1938 Smith and Wesson .38 caliber revolver.

Smith found it wrapped in oiled rags. It was clean, but he didn't trust the ammunition. The shoulder holster was curled and brittle.

He remembered the last time he had used the gun. It was on a drop into France. He was with the old OSS that later became the CIA. He was told to shoot a young woman who was a Nazi collaborator and was going to get them all killed. He remembered how she smiled. She knew he was going to shoot her, and she just smiled as if it were some joke. It haunted him. He spent spare moments for almost a year reassuring himself that he had saved count-less lives by shooting that smiling woman.

Only years later, when he was running the organization, did he understand what had happened. Ironically, it was Remo who made it come clear, in an afterthought, mention-ing how some people—knowing they had lost and sensing they had an amateur in front of them—would laugh or smile as their last striking-out at their killer.

"Chiun tells me some people do that," Remo said.

"Did someone, a target, do that to you recently?" Smith asked.

"Oh, no," Remo had said. "They do it sometimes to amateurs."

"Oh," Smith had said. Remo had become the professional.

And now the professional was off somewhere while the amateur was going to defend the life of the chief executive officer of his nation.

How many hundreds of millions had the country spent for the organization and in return was getting a man who in any other service would have been retired for age and who had found that his shoulder holster had split from age and he was going to have to carry his revolver in his briefcase.

When Irma said good-bye to him—he told her that he was going to Washington for a few days—he saw that she had been crying. She knew he was carrying the gun again.

You didn't stay married to a man for so many years and not know a thing like that.

Chapter Five

The president was overjoyed.

The country had spent $7 billion to develop an antimissile space ray, and that didn't work. The federal government had lent cities $20 billion to repair subways and they didn't work.

Bridges were crumbling around the country, and all the road tax money didn't seem to help them at all. Educational costs had tripled and the only educational increase was in illiteracy across the land.

But this evening, he was going to see more than his money's worth. His predecessor had told him about the old man who could crush glass in his hands, shredding it to powder, and then through finger movement make it into glass again.

The man could climb walls.

His money's worth.

"Sir, your new auxiliary bodyguard is here. But he's, well, sort of old, sir," said the chief of the Secret Service detail assigned to the White House.

"Well, don't mess with him, whatever you do," chuckled the president. He wondered what sort of robes the man would wear. His predecessor had said he wore flowing crimson robes with golden decorations over which his long fingernails seemed to flutter.

This time the man was dressed in a gray three-piece suit. He had a lemony face. He apologized for being a bit late because he had to get ammunition and a new holster.

"You cut your fingernails, I see," said the president. Harold Smith glanced at his fingernails, then shook his head.

"They're short," the president said.

"Yes," Smith agreed.

They were in a private meeting room outside the Oval Office. The president was wearing pajamas and a bathrobe. He was preparing for bed.

"We have information," Smith said, "that someone is going to make another attempt on your life at six A.M. tomorrow. For some reason, the Secret Service failed to get word to you."

"They've been penetrated?" asked the president.

"I don't know. It may be, but it may not. Sometimes things just don't work."

The president sighed and then gave a good-natured smile. "I know all too well. But you're here now."

"What I propose, sir, is that I stay with you until tomorrow's incident passes. Then use alternate bodyguards until I can track down these people who are trying to kill you."

"Do you know who they are?"

"No, sir," Smith said. "But they have made a mistake in using certain communications systems that I can pick up."

"At least there are other people in the world who make mistakes," the president said. Smith was impressed by the man's good nature in the face of adversity and danger.

"Well, good luck," said the president. "But say, could you do me a favor? Would you show me how you shred glass in your fingers?"

"I'm sorry. I can't do that," Smith said.

"Well, then, could you climb a wall?"

"I guess. I used to be able to if there were stepholds."

"No. I mean straight up a sheer wall."

"You're thinking of someone else," Smith said. "He's not available now."

"There's a young white guy who's pretty good too, I was told," the president said.

"He is busy also," Smith said.

"You guys certainly must be doing important things when the president of the United States rates number three on your list."

Smith sat outside the president's private door, along with a young healthy man with a square jaw and an athletic build. The CURE director felt like some uncomfortable subway rider out of place in the great mansion that was the White House, sitting next to a young man who knew he did not belong there.

There was a White House rule that bodyguards were not supposed to talk while on guard because that would distract them. But Smith didn't have to talk with the young man to know what he was thinking every time he glanced over at the late middle-aged man in the three-piece suit with the bulge of a regular size .38 caliber revolver, manufactured in 1938, under his jacket. He could feel the young man wanting to ask Smith where he had bought that cannon that was jammed in under his jacket.

The pistol was almost as big as the young man's Uzi machine pistol, that all-purpose Israeli sidearm so preferred by bodyguards around the world.

Well, the pistol would have to be better than the Uzi.

Because if that young athletic man made a move to the door of the president's sleeping quarters at 6 A.M., Harold W. Smith was going to have to drop him with the .38.

At 5:55 A.M., Smith suddenly realized he had made a mistake. It came when the young man was relieved. And the mistake was not that the young man might be the one who would kill the president. Smith suddenly realized that the president didn't leave his sleeping quarters until 10 A.M., and he was going to be hit while he slept. In his bedroom. Smith made a move to the door, but the new guard's Uzi was suddenly facing his eyes. The barrel was wider when it was pointed at you, he realized.

Smith was past retirement age for many government departments, and he was looking down the barrel of a gun again.

"You cannot enter alone," said the door guard. He was a clean-cut young black man with the darkest, coldest eyes Smith had ever seen. The Secret Service had chosen well.

"I've got to. The president is in danger."

"You cannot enter without permission of the pre-wake shift supervisor."

"Let's get it."

"You know what this can do to your career?" asked the black Secret Service man.

"Call him," said Smith. The Uzi never left Smith's direction as the agent used a wall device to phone his shift supervisor.

"He'll be down in five minutes," the agent said.

"That's too late," Smith said.

"You cannot enter," the bodyguard said. "You can only protect this station."

"Three minutes from now will be too late. We might already be too late."

"I'm sorry. You cannot enter."

Very slowly and without a sudden motion, because it

had to be done slowly, Smith reached his right hand under his jacket and withdrew his pistol between thumb and forefinger. The Uzi raised to Smith's eye. Smith bent and placed the pistol on the carpeting. If he had dropped the old thing, it might have gone off.

Then, with knees creaking, he stood up and said to the Secret Service agent, "You are going to have to kill me to stop me from entering."

"You cannot enter," the agent said.

Smith very slowly turned the handle on the door to the president's sleeping quarters. The large-barreled Uzi went to his right eyeball. He could feel his eye touch the gun metal. It make him blink. In a moment, the great black hole of the barrel would flash, and Smith's head would be splashed all over the White House hallway.

"I am sorry," Smith said. "I have to enter."

And he pushed the door open silently. It opened to a small Georgian living room with the embers of a pre-night fire dying down. The carpeting made no noise under Smith's feet. The agent walked alongside him, the Uzi still pressed to Smith's head.

A large white door with a polished brass handle stood at the right. Smith moved across the carpet and opened the door. He could see the agent's trigger finger tense. If the man hiccupped, that gun was going off.

Smith opened the door. He could hear snoring. It came from a large white canopied bed.

It came from a woman with her eyes shielded by night blinders. A man slept next to her. He looked camera-perfect, even in his sleep.

"Mister President," Smith said. "Get out of that bed. Get out now." The gun still pointed at his head.

"What? What?" said the president. "Who? What? Oh, you. Yes. Yes." The president nudged his wife.

"Dear, you've got to get up."

"I just fell asleep," she said.

"You've got to get up," the president said.

"You really do, ma'am. Right now," Smith said.

"Oh, my god," said the president's wife, covering herself with covers as she sat up with night-blinders on.

"Come quickly," said Smith. The president led her by the hand out of the bed. Smith nodded them toward the door to the hallway, and shut their bedroom door. It was 6 A.M. exactly.

Smith knew the door was very good because it stayed on its hinges as the blast went off behind it. The floor shook.

"My god," said the black Secret Service agent. He lowered the Uzi.

"That was close," said the president. His voice was almost cheerful.

Smith had never seen anyone barely escape death and still exhibit such charm. "Are you all right, sir?" he asked.

"You bet," the president said. "I just started the day a bit earlier."

"How can you be smiling, sir?" Smith asked.

"I'm just imagining how disturbed the press corps is going to be when they find out someone missed again."

"Eeeeek," screamed the president's wife. The agent stepped back as though punched by her scream. Smith looked dumbfounded. Only the president was calm.

"You," she screamed at the president. "You and your frigging good nature. Will you hate, damn you? They almost killed us."

"But they missed," said the president with a smile. He looked around for a jelly bean.

"Hate," she shrieked. "Hate someone. Hate anything. Dammit, will you hate?"

"If it will help you, sure, dear. I'll hate whoever you want me to hate."

"Anyone, damn you," she screamed. Veins bulged in her neck as she turned to Smith. "I've had to live with this damned good nature for thirty years now. Vilification in the press. Daily attacks and now bombs, and that . . . that . . . that whatever-it-is won't hate."

The shift supervisor finally made it down, and there was a confusion of men and guns and walkie-talkies. With the president's consent, Smith took charge.

"Sir, there is no time as safe for you as the next few minutes. Please get dressed. I would like to meet with you and your one most trusted advisor."

"I trust them all," the president said.

"Wouldn't you know?" said his wife. "And you," she said, pointing to Smith. "Why is now so damned safe?"

"Because they've just missed. They think the president is dead. He is safe until they find out he is still alive. Then it becomes dangerous again because they'll try again."

"Good," said the First Lady. "That's something I can deal with. At least there are some reasonably vicious people around. Good. I can hate them."

"You can't blame her," said the president. "It's lousy getting awakened in the middle of the night."

"Yes sir," said Smith.

The man the president chose to accompany him to the meeting with Smith was his secretary of the interior. A bald man who also had a good nature. Smith was grim.

"First, let me thank you for giving me authority here in the White House, but I am going to have to leave you."

"Why?" asked the secretary.

"Because if I stay here, the president is definitely going to die. Eventually, one of these attempts will work. This is not some nut somewhere with a fast shot in a crowd. This is a determined methodical attempt on the president's life."

"Another government?" asked the president.

"I don't know yet. But until we put them away, you are not safe."

"How do you know it's even an organization?" asked the secretary of the interior. "How do we know we're not dealing with one nut?"

"Because they have a communications network. And because we found the person who planted the bomb. She was the chambermaid who made the bed."

"And she said there were others?"

"Most eloquently," Smith said drily. "Her throat was cut by a not too sharp instrument."

The good nature left the face of the president. The secretary of the interior shook his head.

"How can you be sure you can get them before they strike again?" asked the president.

"I can't."

"Then I'm still vulnerable. Other people could get hurt around here if this keeps up," the president said.

"I have a plan to deal with that. Go abroad," Smith said.

"What will that do?" asked the secretary.

"That will get the host country's secret service in charge of the president's safety."

"You mean the president has to leave the country because it's not safe for him to stay here?" the secretary of the interior asked. It was not so much a question as a statement.

"Exactly," said Smith.

"Well, that is one piece of garbage," said the secretary.

"Yes," Smith agreed.

The secretary of the interior's forehead was perspiring. He pulled a handkerchief from his vest pocket, and a few seeds fell from the handkerchief.

"Where did you get those?" Smith snapped.

"Are they back again?" asked the secretary, holding up a seed. It was pale yellow and the size of a gnat.

"It's a grass seed," he said. "They're trying to frighten me. Just some environmentalist nuts."

"Do these people always leave grass seeds around?" Smith asked.

"Yeah. It's their calling card. They believe in the universal goodness of everything. Except people. They are the fringe of fringes. They protest everything."

"When did you put that handkerchief in your pocket?" Smith asked.

"Could you two deal with this later?" the president asked. "We ought to move along with our plans if I'm to leave the country."

"This is why you have to leave the country," Smith said. He took the seeds from the secretary along with the handkerchief. "We found the chambermaid dead. In the ragged edges of her throat were sprinkled a few grass seeds. They may be crazy, Mr. Secretary, but they're not so harmless."

But the secretary of the interior was not listening. At the very moment he realized that the people who had attempted to kill the president had gotten as close to him as his handkerchief, the fear and tension overloaded his nervous system, and he removed himself from the horror of it by simply passing out.

Chapter Six

They called him the Dutchman.

He was an American. His real name had been Jeremiah Purcell, but now 'the Dutchman' suited him as well as any. Long ago, before the madness in him forced him to run endlessly away from the world, he had lived on a small Dutch Caribbean island. The natives there gave him the name. He had tried to isolate himself then, thinking that if he could hide well enough, his powers could be controlled.

But nothing could control what the Dutchman had inside him.

He awoke in the full blaze of afternoon light. He felt a sharp stab of fear, as he did every time he faced a new day.

Where am I?

Squinting into the brilliant sunlight, he made out the conical shapes of the Anatolian lava mountains with their almost absurd-looking little cutout squares where the inhabitants of the area chose to live.

Cappadocia. Now he remembered. He had been in Asia

Minor for three days. Although the name was not to be found on any modern map, the residents of this part of eastern Turkey south of Ankara still called their home by its Biblical name.

He was thirsty. He felt his lips with his fingers. They were dry and cracked. His face was tender. He was fair skinned, and burned easily. He didn't remember falling asleep. Sleep was so rare for him that he was grateful whenever it came, but he wished he hadn't slept where the sun could burn him so badly.

What have I done?

There was a woman . . . blisters . . . a fire . . . Death, death everywhere . . .

Stop it, he told himself. He couldn't change the past.

Or the future. It will all be the same.

Nearby, a farmer led a goat cart filled with containers of milk toward the village. Jeremiah stumbled forward on wobbly legs. The first hours after waking were sometimes painfully sane. At night, when his energies were high, when his mind flew, free and out of control, he could forget. There was no terrible past for him then, no future filled with dread and loathing. But now, and for a few minutes every day, he remembered the freakish thing that he was with an awful clarity.

I am the Dutchman.

Maker of nonexistent worlds, manipulators of minds. Heir to the secrets of Sinanju. Possessor of a power greater than any man should have to bear. The Dutchman, specter of death, fated to live without peace, without rest, until his mission was fulfilled.

He moved on silent feet toward the goat cart. As usual, the animals reared and panicked when they caught his scent, knocking the heavy metal containers on their sides. Animals had always feared him. They understood the disguises of death better than humans did.

But here, among the primitive mountain dwellers of Cappadocia, even the humans knew him. They had seen him kill. They had some idea of the terrible extent of his madness. The farmer fled, screaming. His goats pulled in all directions, their eyes bulging as the Dutchman drew nearer.

He set them free and lifted one of the containers to his lips. The milk was warm but good. He drank greedily.

Something moved. There was a sound like a wail, quickly muffled. With a start, he set down the container and shifted the dried grass inside the cart. At the back, hidden behind the tall containers and half covered with grass, was a thin young woman holding an infant in her arms. Her shoulders shook. With jerky movements, she tried to put the baby behind her. Its fat brown legs kicked out at the air.

He felt something stirring within him. Colors, a strange music, a heightened awareness. The little brown legs seemed to glow, blocking out everything around them.

No, he told himself. He would not let it happen. He had felt the same wild longing nearly all his life. It heralded the unleashing of the inhuman beast he carried inside him. He had watched a pig explode when he was ten years old, and had realized even then that somehow he had made it happen. He was born with the gift of death. He had set his own parents on fire just by imagining it. He had transformed a beautiful girl into a mass of boils with the hideous power of his mind. And now he saw the baby's fat brown legs charred black to the bone, disappearing into ash . . .

The baby cried, jarring his thoughts. It was too late to stop the power, but he could divert it if he . . . tried. . . .

"Go," he shouted in Turkish. "Take the baby. Now."

Feeling as if every muscle and nerve in his body were being ripped apart, he forced his gaze away from the baby and onto one of the uninhabited stone mountains. It had been so difficult, just the slight turning of his head, that he thought he would die from the effort. He knew it would not be long before he would be unable to control the power even that much.

Relaxing, allowing his eyes to rest on the great peak of gray rock, he exhaled slowly. The mountain changed before his eyes to a glowing, jagged mass of electric blue. Dissonant music, sounding like a choir of tormented souls, rose up around him. The mountain glowed green, then orange, outlined with an aura of bright white. The air smelled acrid and oppressive. The power had engulfed the mountain.

"Nuihc, why have you done this to me?" he cried. If he had been left alone, he might have died in childhood, as other mutants did. He should not have been permitted to develop to his capabilities. He should never have been privy to the teachings of Sinanju, which strengthened a mind that was already too strong to live among men. But his teacher, Nuihc, the man who had saved him from the world of men, had not allowed him to die. For Nuihc had seen in young Jeremiah Purcell a being who could help him to conquer the earth. In Jeremiah, Nuihc had created the Dutchman, homeless, mad, doomed. And now Nuihc was dead.

"You may serve me in only one way," Nuihc had said a thousand times before his death.

The Dutchman still remembered the first time he heard the conditions of his life under the strange Oriental teacher.

"How may I serve you, Master?" he had asked.

"Kill him who rules the destiny of Sinanju. Should I die, bring to death by your own hands the Master Chiun. Only then will you find rest."

Kill Chiun. Find the Master of Sinanju and kill him, or live forever in torment.

The distant peak quivered and trembled like a piece of crumpled paper. Then, its sides heaving apart, the mountain exploded in a crash of flying rock that blackened the sky.

When it was over, he fell on the ground and sobbed.

Chapter Seven

Even before Remo got to Peru, he knew that he never wanted to see that country again. It had been the worst trip of his life. The small boat he had set sail in broke apart during a storm in the Sea of Okhotsk. He was picked up near dawn by a Russian freighter, whose captain was going to turn him over to Soviet authorities until Remo uncovered several crates filled with eight-millimeter porno films. The Russian captain didn't understand much English, but "contraband" was a word he understood. So was "Siberia."

Thus was Remo dumped overboard somewhere in the vicinity of the Aleutian Islands, where he was rescued by an American seaplane and carted as far as Juneau, Alaska. Slogging on foot to a U.S. military base some fifty miles away, he stowed away on an experimental supersonic fighter on a test run to Houston. At the Gulf of Mexico, he hitched a ride on a Mexican fishing boat in exchange for labor.

Several thousand mackerel later, he arrived in Merida, Mexico, stinking but richer by twelve dollars—enough to get him on a series of second-class buses crammed to bursting with chickens and pigs, through the middle American countries. It was touch and go at the borders of El Salvador, Nicaragua, Costa Rica, Colombia, and Equador. By the time he arrived in the vast, unpopulated Peruvian highlands, he knew he'd been right. The Master's Trial was an exercise in lunacy. No one would ever find him in this place. He sat beneath a yew tree and slept.

He awoke in the middle of a sea of painted faces. Nearly a hundred men surrounded him, all of them decked out in feathers and tunics of bright cloth. They carried spears. The spears were pointed straight at him.

"Wait a second," Remo said, staggering to his feet. "Whoever you think I am, you're wrong. *Donde est—*" His high school Spanish deserted him. Not that it mattered. He didn't know where he was going, anyway.

He searched his mind for the name of the man he had come to see. Jildo? No, Jildo was the Viking. There was someone named Kirby, or Kibbee, and then the guy in Wales, Emory or something. Why didn't these people have ordinary names?

"Me Remo," he said, pulling out his jade stone.

The leader of the group took it out of his hand and examined it. He nodded to the others, then gave it back, motioning Remo forward.

"Ancion," Remo said, remembering. "That's the name of the guy I'm supposed to meet."

At the mention of the name, the warriors all laid down their spears and knelt. "Ancion," they chanted, bowing low.

"Ancion must be a big cheese."

"Ancion," they intoned.

They walked for half a day through the hills, over a rope bridge spanning a large river, and finally up a narrow footpath winding in a spiral around a high mountain. At the apex was a bank of stone steps leading to a massive building painted brightly and adorned with carved friezes. In the floor outside the main entrance was a smooth, domed rock bearing the same three characters as Remo's rock. The warrior leader took Remo inside, into a large stone chamber. In addition to the warriors, more than a hundred others were present, kowtowing toward a gold throne placed atop a pyramid of steps twenty feet high. On it sat a young man with refined, chiseled features. He was dressed in a checkered tunic weighted heavily with gold and silver, and a cape of what Remo recognized as bat fur. He wore a wide band of colored cloth around his head, and two large gold discs five inches wide over his ears. In his hand was a feathered scepter.

The warrior who had brought Remo held out his hand and slapped the palm with two fingers. Uncertain of what he wanted, Remo gave him the piece of jade. It seemed to satisfy the warrior. He presented it to the man on the throne.

"You are the heir to the Master of Sinanju?" the one in bat fur asked. "A white man?"

"Nobody's perfect," Remo said. "Are you Ancion?"

"Ancion," the crowd murmured.

"Is that the only word they know?"

The eyes of the man on the throne flashed. "The name of the Inca is sacred. It is not to be spoken by outsiders."

Remo looked around. "Which Inca?"

"There is but one Inca. He who rules the Inca peoples, descended from a hundred generations of kings. Our ways are not like yours, where even a mongrel white American is designated to take the place of the Master of Sinanju." He stared at Remo contemptuously. "Do not dare to use my name again."

Remo fought down the urge to jog up the stairs and punch Ancion in the nose. "Whatever makes you happy," he said. "Say, whoozis, it's about this fight we're supposed to have."

"The Master's Trial is not a 'fight.' "

"Well, it's not exactly a tea party. Look, You may not know this, but I'm supposed to kill you."

Ancion smiled coldly. "If you can, white man."

"Okay, okay. Maybe you'll kill me. The point is, this makes about as much sense as a circle jerk at the North Pole. Let's talk it over, okay?"

"If you are afraid to fight me, then acknowledge your defeat."

"Fine," Remo said. "You're the winner. Congrats. See you in church." He ambled away.

"Stop," Ancion shouted.

"What now? I told you you won."

"In the Master's Trial, only the victor lives. If you will not fight, you will be executed."

Remo said, "Hey, what's with you, anyway? I'm offering you an easy way out. We've both got better things to do than beat each other up like a couple of Tenth Avenue hoods. I just want to talk."

"The talking was done twelve centuries ago. Make your choice. The arena or the gallows?"

The man's English was definitely accented, but the accent wasn't Spanish. "How come you sound just like the Kennedys?" Remo asked.

"I was educated at Harvard. What is your choice, white man?"

"Harvard? Did they teach you there that it's okay to murder strangers?"

"I went to your country to study the ways of so-called civilized men. What I found was that civilization breeds war above all other things."

"And what do you think the Master's Trial breeds, hamsters?"

''What we do today is not war, but a sacred tradition to avert war among the great remaining societies of the world. Without the Master's Trial, our peoples would fight one another openly. We would become known to the outside world. We would be absorbed into the huge, useless nations of the planet, wallowing in mediocrity. Without our traditions, we would lose our past. Do you not understand?''

''We don't have to fight each other in the first place,'' Remo said. ''We can just mind our own business.''

''That is not the nature of our peoples.''

''How do you know? This dumb contest's been going on for a thousand years. Maybe ten thousand. Maybe we ought to try and get along.''

''This is a useless argument,'' Ancion said. ''We are not here to abolish the Master's Trial.''

''Why not?''

''What is your choice, coward?''

Remo sighed. ''I'll fight you,'' he said at last. ''What a pain in the ass you are.''

As the Inca rose, the people in the room prostrated themselves on the floor. Ancion glided regally down the long staircase to a covered palanquin held by four stocky men on their knees. At a signal, they rose and carried Ancion outside.

Remo followed him into a stone amphitheater on the grounds behind the palace. Ancion's subjects, numbering nearly a thousand now, gathered around to watch.

''What happens if I win?'' Remo asked, indicating the crowd.

''They will only kill you if you use magic.''

''You learned a lot of terrific things at Harvard.''

''They will watch for sorcery,'' Ancion said. An aide handed him what looked like a large ball made of leather strips.

"I hate to break it to you, but there's no such thing as sorcery," Remo said.

The Inca didn't look at him. "Now I see you are ignorant as well as arrogant."

"Knock it off, Ancion."

"Ancion," the crowd chanted.

"Will you guys cut that out?" Remo yelled. "So I'm ignorant because I don't believe in magic, huh? Well, this isn't the Middle Ages, you know. Which is what I've been trying to tell you since I got here."

"There is sorcery," Ancion said. "If you do not recognize it, then it will defeat you."

"Oh, I see. Is that what you're going to do, put the old whammy on me?"

"I have no magic," Ancion said quietly. "H'si T'ang has. The Other has."

Remo started. "The Other?"

"The one of legend, whom only magic can conquer."

"What's his name?"

"He has no name. He is the Other. But you will not meet him, because I will kill you first."

He grasped the end of a leather string protruding from the ball in his hands and snapped his arm outward. The ball unraveled with a crack into a long whip ending in a baseball-sized sphere that glittered with green light. It sang as Ancion twirled it above his head.

"My weapon is a *bola* of cut emeralds in mortar. What is yours?"

Remo watched the flying stone twirl in expert figure-eights in the sky. He knew by its speed that it could slice him in two in a fraction of a second. Ancion's face was set in deadly earnest. There was no way to talk him out of the Master's Trial now.

"What is your weapon?" the Inca repeated.

Remo readied himself, relaxing his muscles, focusing his energy, preparing his mind. "Sinanju," he said.

The crowd hushed. Ancion's bola whistled as it swung low, the first attack. Remo leaped over it. The Inca turned effortlessly, keeping the sparkling green ball taut at a distance of ten feet between himself and Remo. Then, the whip advancing like a snake, the second attack came. Small fluttering circles that sent Remo flying backward. When Remo was almost at the edge of the spectators, Ancion pulled the bola back into a huge, shrieking ellipse that cut through the air at different levels on each lightning-fast rotation.

The ball came at Remo's knees, then his neck, then his stomach. There was no way to get close to Ancion, unless he timed his attack with the rhythm of the bola. He waited, he counted. He felt the beating of the sailing ball, and prepared himself to advance when it was farthest from him. Then he moved quickly, straight ahead.

In the split second before he went down, Remo saw the hint of a smile on Ancion's face. For in that moment, just as Remo's feet twitched to advance forward, the Inca changed the rhythm of the flying weighted whip in his hand. With a jerk he shortened the length of leather cord. Before Remo could react to the movement, he felt the cut gems slit three deep grooves in his back.

"Are you still so sure you will kill me, American?" He pulled the bola back.

Remo got to his feet, feeling the throb in the flesh of his back. "Why—why didn't you kill me? You had the chance."

"The Master's Trial is a contest of skill, not a massacre. I will not harm a man on the ground." He swung the weapon forward.

Remo dodged it, but barely. It came at him again. He rolled, scattering the crowd. Again he was on the ground, and again Ancion stepped back, waiting. His aristocratic features were impassive.

Who is this man? Remo thought. Ancion had sworn to kill him, and yet he had spared his life twice in five minutes. This wasn't the kind of fighting Remo was used to. It was clean. It was fair. And it was good. Weapon or no weapon, Ancion knew how to handle himself.

"All right," Remo said. "You've made your point."

Ancion moved in, the bola forming a complex pattern in the air.

"I mean it. You're too good to be wasted."

"Get up," Ancion said contemptuously. "At least have the courage to die like a man."

Remo blinked. It had not occurred to him before that he might die. No one had ever been good enough to scare him, really scare him, in years. But Ancion was.

The bola sped by Remo's face. He swallowed. He couldn't move in forward. Ancion knew all those tricks. And he couldn't get to him from behind, because Ancion could control that, too. He had to stop . . . *the arm.* The easy, effortless swinging had to stop first. Then they could talk. Or something. Just stop the arm . . .

The bola came around on another pass. Remo waited. On the third, he leaped directly over the ball into a backward spin and landed hard on the Inca's shoulder. The bola spun wildly, but it never left Ancion's grasp. Remo arched backward, out of the way, as Ancion jerked the leather whip in crazy directions. His shoulder was broken, but he kept the weapon moving.

"Stop it!" Remo shouted. "You're hurt."

With a cry of pain, Ancion thrust the bola out once more.

The people watching scrambled out of the way. The ball hit a rock and careened backward at tremendous speed,

thudding into Ancion's chest. With a groan, the Inca
dropped to the ground.

Remo went to him. Ancion's chest was exploded open,
the blood pouring in rhythmic spurts from the large wound.

"Where's a doctor?" Remo shouted.

"They do not understand your language," Ancion said
slowly. "There is no need, anyway." He closed his eyes,
then opened them again. "You were not a coward, after
all."

"I've never seen anyone fight like you before," Remo
said.

The Inca shifted painfully. "You will," he said. "The
opponents of the Master's Trial are worthy, as you are
worthy. You used no magic."

"I don't have magic," Remo said.

"Then beware. The Other has magic. The Other will
come for you. This is the year. He will come."

"I'm not going to fight anyone else."

"You must. It is the law of the Master's Trial. The
other warriors will be killed by their people if you do not
fight them, after vanquishing me. It will be a grave insult."

Remo couldn't believe his words. "Are you saying
you're glad this happened?"

"It was fair," Ancion said. "I die honorably. That is all
any warrior can ask."

Remo slipped his arms beneath the Inca's back. "I'll
take you inside," he said.

"No. Leave me here. My people will see to me. They
have buried their kings for five thousand years." His head
fell back.

Remo rose, looking at the lifeless body of Ancion.
There was a soft rumbling among the crowd of spectators.

"Hold it," Remo said to the advancing mob. "This was
his idea, not mine."

The man Remo recognized as the warrior who led him

to the palace stepped forward and fell on his knees before him. The others bowed, too, until Remo was surrounded by kneeling subjects.

Remo stared at them, horrified. "Get up!" he shouted. "Can't you see I've just killed your king? What's wrong with all of you?"

But no one moved. The law of the Master's Trial had prevailed.

Disgusted, he picked his way through the prostrate bodies of the people and walked away. He never looked back.

Chapter Eight

Sinanju.

It was the only purpose in the Dutchman's life now, a beacon signaling in the darkness.

Find Chiun. Find Nuihc's sworn enemy. Then he would find rest.

The moon was full, its light coating the budding trees in the Russian steppes where he walked. He had already come a thousand miles, but he felt no fatigue. Nuihc's training had seen to that.

Nuihc had himself been trained to become Master of Sinanju, following the reign of Chiun, his uncle. He had spent a lifetime of preparation learning the intricacies of the most difficult and effective of the martial arts. But Chiun had cast him out of the village before the title of Master could be bestowed on him.

Nuihc spent the rest of his life trying to regain the legacy that was rightfully his, but Chiun had bested him again and again. Even in his old age, the Master of Sinanju had devised a secret weapon against Nuihc. He trained another pupil, an American, to carry out his will.

The Dutchman had heard Nuihc's story many times. His teacher had grown bitter and spiteful with failure. The disappointment of being cheated out of his destiny aged him before his time. Whenever Nuihc told the story, his eyes would glint with hatred.

And triumph. For even with his own skills lessened by the gnawing hate for his uncle, Nuihc had found a way to avenge Chiun's unfairness.

He got the idea when he heard of Chiun's new protegee. It was a perfect plan, a way to ensure his success even if he himself were to die. He would find his own heir, another to whom he would teach all the secrets of Sinanju that he had learned from Chiun.

But this heir could not be an ordinary man, as Chiun's was. The legacy of Nuihc would go only to one so powerful that neither Chiun nor his American "son" could defeat him. He searched around the world for such an heir. And one day, on a train in the plains of Iowa, he found him.

Jeremiah Purcell was just a boy then, but a boy such as Nuihc had never seen. He could direct others to do his will without speaking a word. An amazing boy who could set people on fire by thought alone.

The boy was a freak, doomed to a life of imprisonment, a laboratory rat whose tremendous power would be studied and written about behind glass walls. The boy himself had wanted to die, even at the age of ten.

But Nuihc changed everything. He took Jeremiah away from civilization and nurtured him. He secretly taught him the entire discipline of Sinanju. The boy was a magnificent pupil, made even more formidable by the dangerous abilities of his mind. And if those abilities caused the boy to suffer, it was of no concern to him. Jeremiah was a weapon, not a son to be coddled.

Nuihc protected himself from his creation by staying

away from the boy as much as possible, teaching him the methods of killing that were the essence of Sinanju, and then leaving him to practice alone for months on end. As Jeremiah grew, his exercises became more difficult. Nuihc would absent himself for years at a stretch, returning only to check on the boy's progress and remind him of the debt he owed him.

Should I die, bring to death by your own hands the Master Chiun.

And then, after years of silence, Jeremiah learned that Nuihc was dead. The mission of his life had begun.

He panicked. He was still too young. He took himself to the small Dutch island to train with all the power at his disposal. He ranged his mind along the empty seacoast, perfecting its destructiveness. But something began to happen, something he had not counted on. The more he used his mind, the more he needed the awesome horror it begat. The episodes of mental work left him exhausted and frightened, but he couldn't stop. As the madness grew, it overtook his sanity.

He needed to kill, the way he needed to breathe. The power became an overwhelming thing, a wild beast that lived inside him, uncontrollable, unpredictable. He had to learn how to rein it in, make it manageable, before the beast destroyed him. He needed time.

Time was the one thing he didn't have. By sheerest accident, Chiun and his pupil came to the island, and the Dutchman met his destiny.

He was too young. It had come to nothing. He failed to carry out Nuihc's demand. He had not found the rest he so needed. He traveled around the world, confused and terrified. The beast had won. He was helpless in its presence.

Until Cappadocia. Then he knew. It was time. The beast was going to destroy him anyway. Perhaps he would find

Chiun before it did. Perhaps, once he accomplished his task, he would be free.

As long as he did not allow the madness to take root, he reminded himself. *Keep the beast caged, and you'll find your way.* He took pains to keep away from civilization. *No people.* People were too strong a temptation for the beast. It needed to kill, and once it started, it couldn't stop.

He foraged for his food. He ate no meat, drank nothing but water. He walked and ran each day toward the east until he fell with exhaustion. The days were long, his periods of rest short. He made good time.

Keep the beast caged. . . .

He heard a sound. In the leaves on the forest floor behind him were footsteps, small and unself-conscious. A girl's voice sang a pretty Russian folk tune.

He ran.

"Ho," the girl called, laughing.

He closed his eyes in despair. It was already too late.

She was young, no more than twenty, with dark, curly hair and smiling eyes. She wore a red shawl over her dress and carried in her hands a basket filled with mushrooms. "Are you lost?" she asked in Russian.

The language was familiar to him, as nearly all were. Part of his training had been to learn every major language spoken on earth. It had been the easiest part of his schooling, and the most pleasurable.

"I'm—I'm just walking," he said.

It had been so long since he'd held a woman. Mixed with the fragrance of the forest, he could smell her, warm and sweet and female.

"Do you live in the village?" she asked, smiling. It was an invitation.

He tried to talk, to utter some pleasantry and then depart, but his eyes couldn't leave hers.

"I said—"

He stepped forward and took her in his arms.

She intoxicated him. Her lips were ripe and hot. The skin on her neck was as smooth as alabaster. Beneath it, blue veins throbbed with her heartbeat.

She pulled away from him in a tease. He was a handsome man, lean and tall, with eyes of an extraordinary electric blue color, and women liked him. Women who didn't know what he was.

"Please go," he whispered.

She laughed. "Are you frightened? No one will see us." Setting down her basket, she unknotted the shawl around her shoulders and let it slip to the ground. Beneath her dress he could see the outline of her erect nipples in the bright moonlight. She held out her hands to him, sturdy working hands that knew how to please a man. A prostitute, he thought.

"How much?"

"No more than a few kopeks. For my family. You will not regret it." She smoothed her hands over him, lingering expertly over the growing hardness between his legs. "You will please me, too."

She undressed him and put her mouth on him. He closed his eyes and allowed the colors to wash over him. Bright, familiar colors . . . The beast was unlocking its cage and stretching its muscles.

He groaned. "Stop . . . you must stop."

"But I've just begun," she teased. Her tongue flicked over him as softly as a moth's wings.

The beast was laughing at him. It would never be caged again.

With a yank, he pulled her up by her hair and tore her dress from top to bottom. She shrieked.

"Look what you've done! You are too rough. My dress . . ."

He slapped her, knocking her to the ground. She lay there, stunned, her ripped clothing spread out behind her. Her breasts were large, and quivered with her short, frightened breathing. Her legs were covered by an absurd pair of long cotton bloomers.

As he watched her, she backed away slowly, on her elbows. "Please," she said, holding up one hand as she tried to get to her feet.

He fell on her, pinning her arms over her head, tearing off the pants she wore while she lashed her legs. The struggle enflamed him. When she cried out, he slapped her, again and again, until her face was swollen and bruised. At last she stopped, her wide, terrified eyes spilling over with silent tears.

He entered her in a frenzy, thrusting wildly. She screamed with the pain.

"The police will come for you. My brothers will come—"

He slammed his fist into her mouth. Two teeth broke with a crack and lodged in the back of her throat. She choked, gagging and spitting blood on his face.

He stopped, shaking. The blood. He could taste it. Deadly nectar for the beast.

The girl's eyes rolled back in her head. She stopped struggling, and her clenched fists opened. A sound, deep and rasping, came from her throat. Her blood-smeared mouth froze into an open O.

The Dutchman exploded.

With his teeth, he gouged the blue vein, no longer throbbing, in her neck, and pressed his lips to it, sucking the red juice while he spilled his own fluid into her.

In the distance, a tree cracked and splintered apart in a shower of sparks. The small animals of the forest shrieked and darted for cover.

When he was done, it was nearly dawn. The round moon was high in the graying sky. On the forest floor lay the dead girl's body, caked with dried blood, her face unrecognizable. Beside her were the silly cotton bloomers, now dark with blood.

He staggered away. There was no remembrance, no regret. The ravaged body in the woods meant nothing to him. The beast had won. In the Dutchman's mind was only a feeling of deep, everlasting weariness, and one thought. A word: Sinanju.

Chapter Nine

As the president of the United States was flying to Europe for a special meeting with the German president, Harold Smith was attending his first lecture sponsored by the Earth Goodness Society.

Its president was a British physician named Mildred Pensoitte, who was speaking to a school assembly at Revvers College in Massachusetts, where just days before, the American ambassador to the United Nations had not been allowed to speak because her views did not coincide with those of the Revvers english and sociology departments.

As one female student explained to the middle-aged man in the three-piece gray suit:

"We keep bad things from being said here. We have freedom of speech. Some things just shouldn't be said."

"No doubt," said Smith.

"We do have freedom of speech. I disagree all the time. Some of us think America is the most evil nation in history. But then there's the opposite view. Others think it's the second most evil. They think Nazi Germany was the most evil. What do you think?"

"I think many good people died, young lady, so you would have the freedom and comfort to be so absurdly stupid," said Smith who did not usually bother with retorts like that.

The first thing Smith noticed about Revvers College was the vast green lawns and magnificent trees. The second thing he noticed was the vast number of expensive cars. The third thing he noticed were the obscene scrawlings in day-glo paint, calling for an end to manicured lawns and expensive cars.

Dr. Mildred Pensoitte was a handsome woman in her mid-thirties. She spoke in clear tones, making grammatical statements.

There was the earth, she told her enraptured audience. And the earth was good. Everything about it was good. The air was good, or had been once. The grass was pure, or had been once. And the rain was good. Or had been, once.

"And then something happened. Then people who did not care whether anything of the earth, other than their bank accounts, survived, began poisoning it all. We broke our basic contract with nature. And what is that contract, that simple obvious contract? That we are a part of it. A part of nature.

"What right do we have to assume that, just because we can make lawns, we have a right to kill the grass's natural growth? What right do we have to poison the air for all living things? What right do we have to carve the coal from the earth's tender skin and then burn it into poisoned fumes? What right does man-centered man have to murder anything he wishes to help his bank account?"

But Dr. Pensoitte did not hate all men. Only a few men—those who ran America. Not included in Dr. Pensoitte's hates were men who burned people. After all, hadn't the Nazis tried to destroy America? And the Khmer

Rouge, which slaughtered tens of thousands of their own kind—didn't they have a right to mass murder because an American secretary of state once tried to bomb the murderers and didn't confess it all to American reporters before the bombers took off?

At the end, one student stood up and asked, "If America is such a rotten place, why is everyone trying to get in? And if those socialist countries are so good, why is everyone trying to get out?"

There were a few boos. Some of the students said that they wished they had known the other student was going to ask that question so that they could walk out and not listen to it.

But Dr. Pensoitte's cool beauty rode above the anger. She wove a tale of poor, one-crop countries, struggling against imperialistic America. She turned lands that had always had famines into lands that now, somehow, only had famines because of America. Anything the Third World did was a natural right because Americans owned more than one shirt.

Therefore any disasters of socialism were not the fault of socialism but of capitalism. Smith had heard similar reasoning by Nazis against Jews, by Khomeini against Satan, and from fringe preachers about radio stations that wouldn't let them broadcast nonsense without paying for it first.

It was the old devil theory very prominent in the Dark Ages and now with major liberal columnists. It was the new alchemy, the new attempt to make gold from lead, the one piece of thing that would explain everything.

Being young, Smith realized, most of Dr. Pensoitte's audience had not have enough time on earth to realize the nonsense of such simplicity.

She was still talking.

"It is not surprising that a country which would make

enough atomic weapons to destroy the world seven times over would not leave the grass alone. Would someone here tell me how it improves earth to level the grass?''

There were condescending chuckles.

"We not only level grass with hand-pushed rotating blades. We have machines that can do it and poison the air at the same time. We burn electricity from nuclear reactors to do it. And what for? Has the world ever been made one jot better for grass growing in one direction rather than another?''

More chuckles.

"Grass itself is not the problem, of course," Dr. Pensoitte said. "It's the symbol. The person who feels compelled to reduce the earth's growth for the convenience of his feet is precisely the sort of person who has caused all the misery in the world.''

Applause.

"We didn't have atomic bombs and acid rain in the Ice Age and we didn't have something else. We didn't have lawns. We didn't have exploitation by madmen. We didn't have the sort of secretary of the interior who daily rapes your mother, the earth.''

"Mother raper," screamed one student. He had read that the secretary of the interior was going to allow copper mining right in the center of the mingus worm population of South Dakota, perhaps one of the finest mingus worm concentrations in the world. He had been outraged that man would take it upon himself to decide arbitrarily that 14,000 jobs were more important than one of the finest sub-earth cultures in the western hemisphere.

The mingus worm would attach itself to itself and feed on its own excrement for months at a time, forming perhaps one of the finer ecological units on the earth, destroying nothing, using nothing, polluting nothing.

Into the concentration of innocent worms, the secretary of the interior had ordered the killing blades of tractors, gouging the skin of the world for profit. The young man had tried to throw himself in front of a tractor, tried to explain to the tractor operator exactly what he was doing to the earth and then was arrested by the police lackies of the state who so crudely accused him of thinking—the young man remembered the words even as he screamed out support for Dr. Mildred Pensoitte—"a shit-eating worm is more important than a man's job."

"Mother raper. Mother raper," screamed the young man, and the students joined in as the secretary's name was mentioned. The chant had a beat. The chant had a fury. The chant had the confidence of the righteous, sure of the power of their numbers, sure of the inevitability of their triumph, sure of the simple genius of their leader.

Harold W. Smith had heard the chant before. Only the words were different. The words then were "*Seig Heil*."

He was sure of it now. He had come to the right place to look for killers.

Dr. Pensoitte held up something between two fingers. Her voice was soft and innocent. Hitler too knew how to raise and lower the level of his voice, even though the newsreel films only showed him yelling. Hitler had his Jews; Dr. Pensoitte had the American government as embodied in the secretary of the interior.

"And so we use as our symbol the seed of the lowly blade of grass. It was here before capitalism under the hands of white men and it will be here, God willing, when they no longer abuse the earth . . . when they learn quite simply the obvious fact that we are not consumers of the earth, but part of the earth."

There was a hush among the students, and then one started to clap. It unleashed the flow of dammed-up adoration.

Harold W. Smith clapped too. He clapped very hard. He was working.

"She's beautiful, isn't she?" said a girl next to Smith.

"Yes," he said.

Mildred Pensoitte was smiling, cool, content. She had dark brown eyes and high cheekbones and a neck that enhanced the pearls around it.

"Yes. Very beautiful," Smith said.

Dr. Pensoitte was, of course, mobbed after her speech, so Smith couldn't get to her there.

And he realized it would not be easy to get to her at all. The problem with getting to her was that she and her organization, at this time, had no needs. Earth Goodness was oversubscribed with money and had no shortage of volunteers.

Yet without penetrating the organization, he might never find the killer group that had been in Virginia.

He called the Folcroft computers and got good news and bad news. The good news was that after the failure of the second attempt, they would not risk another attempt until the president was back in the country. The bad news was that they would try as soon as he landed.

If only Remo were here. He could get Dr. Pensoitte talking from her ears and nose. He would be on the trail of the killer team within the hour, and once he had them, that would be that.

If Remo were here.

If Remo were there, thought Smith, he could probably seduce Dr. Pensoitte. If he were there, he could penetrate the organization as easily as he did Dr. Pensoitte. He was so good at it, he probably didn't realize it because he didn't even have to stop to think about it.

Smith got a room in Dr. Pensoitte's motel. He phoned to tell her how he admired her organization. He got a male secretary who noted his admiration but would not put him on the telephone with Dr. Pensoitte. Smith said he had a large contribution to make. The male secretary gave him an address to mail it to.

He casually wandered into where she was having dinner among admirers. He smiled and sat down among the very large group and was asked who he was.

"Harry Smith. Fertilizer manufacturer looking to become part of the earth instead of a consumer of it."

"This is a private party," he was told. Dr. Pensoitte did not even look at him.

No entry there.

He came to the Earth Goodness Society with a $5,000 check. He got a thank you. He did not get an invitation to speak to Dr. Pensoitte in person.

He called his computers, but there were no new messages from the killer group. He tried Remo again but didn't get him. He left another message for Chiun but Chiun didn't call back.

And the president was ready to come home any day now. He was running out of excuses to stay in Europe. If he did so much longer, Russia would be sure he was planning a new world war. Nothing else would keep him overseas that long.

Dr. Pensoitte checked out of the motel, and Harold W. Smith was left with a breakfast of prune whip yogurt, a half grapefruit, black coffee, dry toast, and a morning newspaper talking about the strange attacks at the White House and the mysterious sudden presidential trip to Europe.

The Earth Goodness workers to whom he had given his $5,000 came into the motel restaurant with two shoe boxes. They were talking happily. Revvers College had been a good stop for Dr. Pensoitte. There was over $40,000 collected, and that didn't include the heavy contributions in checks. No wonder they hadn't been impressed with Smith's $5,000. And no wonder they didn't have money problems.

In one shoe box, they kept the bankbook and all donations. In the other shoebox, they kept a list of new members' names. When they got back to their office in Washington, D.C., they would have a little old woman type out the new names by hand and put them on addressograph plates. Every few months, when they got around to it, they would send out appeals for money. Receipts for expenditures were kept in an old Jobbo Cleanser barrel. Just before tax time, they would take the barrel down to an accounting service in a discount chain store and have the man do the Earth Goodness Society's books for the year. It cost a hundred dollars and occasionally, they would be a few hundred dollars off the mark in receipts. Every year they had enough money though to sponsor a $½ million rally and a $4 million television education show.

The excess millions were left to grow.

In brief, they were as stable as a seabed.

All this Smith picked up while pretending to read his paper and listening to them complain about how they were really disorganized. They were disorganized, said one of the girls, because they had lost one receipt from the day before.

She was talking about a factor of less than five dollars. Smith dropped his hotel spoon into the yogurt and moved in on this one dangling thread.

He introduced himself as the man who had donated $5,000 the day before. One of the girls remembered him. Somewhat.

"I'd like to help," Smith said. "I see you have problems with receipts, and that's just what I'm good at. I'm retired pretty much, and I would love to do the scut work for you. You need to be freed for the bigger things, the things only young people can do right.''

"You've been listening in on our conversation," said one.

"I have," Smith admitted. "I'm just sort of an old bookkeeper sort. I've done a lot of harm to this earth in my lifetime, and if I can make it up by helping you, in just little things, I would be deeply grateful.''

"We already have a bookkeeper.''

"I'll be her assistant. I'll be a gofer. You've got to let me make up for desecrating Mother Earth. I've been such a human about it.''

"I don't know. We kind of run sort of well now.''

"You're too important to run sort of well. You've got to run perfectly. Your minds have got to be freed from the drudgery of receipt taking and motel room planning. Let it be planned for you.''

"But that's our job.''

"Your job is to save the world from people like the one I used to be. I took the blessings of the earth and made artificial fertilizer to inject into earth's sacred skin so someone could make money. I'm so ashamed.''

As he said this, Smith was making an adjustment in the box listing new members. He noticed one corner of the lid wasn't on right. When he adjusted it, it accidentally fell off and the entire box was a mess. "Let me straighten it out,'' he volunteered. By lunch he was making their hotel reservations, and by supper, he had made his major breakthrough.

They were going to let him give them full and easy access to all their information, immediately, through the use of a computer. Mailing lists were going to go out at the flick of a switch. Receipts would be called up with the touch of another switch. They would have versatility and easy power such as they had never dreamed of.

He even got a thank you call from Dr. Pensoitte herself. But she got off the phone quickly and didn't know his name. It didn't matter. He was on his way. In three days, she would be clinging to his arm for help, and she was going to be helpless without him, her closest advisor. And then he would find out where in the organization a killer arm lurked, and he would intercept it and attack.

He got a mainline computer into their Washington office in the morning before the bookkeeper arrived. Since the little old lady wasn't capable of programming the computer or entering the records, there had to be programmers.

With programmers, of course, there came a personnel director and a personnel committee. There also had to be special programs designed precisely to make Earth Goodness more cost-effective. That used only a few hundred thousand dollars of the surplus.

Instead of Earth Goodness dipping into the bank account to pay all medical bills, Smith drew up a medical program with program director, a minority program, a citizens' awareness program, a rehabilitation program for criminals and, of course, security guards, which he explained were always a necessity when you had a rehabilitation program.

But he was still only nibbling away at the hundreds of thousands. There were millions yet to consume, and a whole day was gone.

It was not until he got the army and navy to help that the battle was won.

Because everything was at their fingertips in the form of a computer identification system for employees, who now numbered over 200, the original Earth Goodness staff in Washington had no more idea of who they were hiring than if they had tried to read the names in the stars.

The Admiral of the Fleet and the Lieutenant General

arrived at Earth Goodness on the day of their retirement from the armed services. Smith gave them one instruction.

"Gentlemen, I am trying to conserve money. Therefore, I will give you only half of anything you ask for. But other than that, you are in charge. Make us lean and mean. Cut costs to the bone."

Within two days, under the leadership of these service academy graduates, Earth Goodness, Inc. was $42 million in debt, and if they cut back all programs by half the next year, they would be running a $127 million deficit. It cost forty dollars every time the toilet was flushed, and the lowest bid on an office throw rug was $13,782.58, and that did not include delivery, which was extra.

But to make sure there was no climbing out of the hole, Smith cut off all chances of retreat. He retired the little old lady and her addressograph cards. He threw out the Jobbo barrel and retained the most prestigious law firm in Washington for a crash organization program.

Once these people had put their minds to it, there was no way to get back to simple management, even with the Jobbo barrel. The lawyers created the grand illusion that with them on hand, somehow all the chaos would be manageable.

The true nature of the disaster, however, was not lost on Dr. Mildred Pensoitte. Just as Smith had planned.

"My lord, we have to launch a giant fund-raising campaign just to buy the stamps to launch another fund-raising campaign. We're running around in circles, and if we stop, we'll be crushed."

At that moment, a very conservative lemon-faced man in a three-piece gray suit walked into her New York City offices with a plan to absolutely, brutally cut everything in half no matter who or what was destroyed. Fire, discharge, close down, cut back, no matter what. He was an expert at it, he assured her.

His named was Harry Smith, he said.

She took one look at that cold, bitter face and strictly parted white hair and knew that he would do just what he promised.

"Call me Mildred," said Dr. Pensoitte.

Chapter Ten

Africa,'' Remo muttered.

Chiun couldn't choose someone for Remo to fight in Ohio. First Peru, then freaking central Africa.

He walked for miles along a bone-dry dirt road into a village where the thatch-and-earth houses seemed to grow like trees out of rock cliffs. It was the third such village he had been to in the Dogon country of Mali, but smaller by half than the other two.

He was looking for a man named Kiree. Nearly everyone he had talked to was familiar with the name, but no one had seen him.

"The greatest among the Dogon," he had been told. Some said that the warrior was old and wise and lived in the middle of the earth. Others insisted that Kiree was a spirit who only materialized when his people were in need. Some of the older villagers thought he was a giant whose footprints had created the sheer cliff faces of the countryside. And there were some who said that Kiree wasn't a man at all, but an insect.

Great, Remo thought. *Here I am in the wilds of Africa to talk sense to a beetle.*

Maybe this is Chiun's idea of a joke. See how far he can jerk me around.

But no. There was Ancion. For the Inca, the Master's Trial had been serious, serious enough to die for. Remo would try again with Kiree, but he wasn't optimistic about the outcome. These people wanted to fight. It didn't make sense, but then nothing about this whole spooky business made much sense.

He stopped in his tracks. Ahead, in a small clearing, a group of men wearing fifteen-foot-high wooden masks and dressed in bizarre costumes of shells and grass skirts danced and shouted in a circle. Apart from them, a few grizzled old men the color of ebony picked at the raw carcass of a goat with their fingers. Musicians played on flutes and drums while gyrating dancers, brightly decorated with exaggerated wooden breasts to resemble women, wove through their column.

Onlookers clapped and chanted as they emerged from the precariously balanced houses on the cliffs. They were a striking people, very tall and long-limbed, with large eyes. The women, their heads draped with colorful turbans, wore silver hoops through their noses.

"Excuse me," Remo asked a group of passersby bedecked in yellow beads. "Can you tell me what's going on?"

The people, all taller than Remo by a head, smiled politely and spoke something that sounded vaguely like water going down a drain.

"I'm looking for someone," he said, pronouncing each word carefully.

The natives laughed apologetically and waved, talking the same incomprehensible tongue.

Remo exhaled noisily, wiping some grime off his face. Another bum steer. This town was your standard African backwater. The other villages he'd passed through at least had donkeys in the streets. There were nothing but scrawny dogs here, along with the dancing Africans.

It must have been hotter than a hundred degrees. Remo felt a rising tide of irritation inside him. How many more dusty, dry villages would he have to visit before the elusive Kiree finally acknowledged his presence? Mali was a big place.

"Thanks anyway," he said to the group wearing the beads. He made the universal gesture of resignation. The Africans nodded and ambled away.

"Are you searching for something?" a voice said in English, seemingly from out of nowhere.

Remo looked around. The only person near him was a dwarf who stood as high as Remo's belt buckle.

"Kind of," Remo said. "A guy named Kiree. You ever hear of him?"

The dwarf shrugged. "One hears many things." He pointed to the dancers. "Would you like to join the funeral?"

"Funeral? That? Looks like a party."

The dwarf smiled as he led Remo past the gathering throng of women on the outer circle of the festivities toward the clearing where the dancers performed. "The Dogon do not believe in death the way westerners do. For them, it is a time of celebration when the spirit leaves, because it will be born again in another, stronger body. Ah, here comes the *dannane*, the hunter."

A dancer in a fierce-looking black mask, clothed in rags and straw, sprang out from behind a spreading bala tree to stalk imaginary prey. "It is hoped that the spirit of the departed will come to rest in the body of one who will grow to be a fine hunter and warrior, like him." He laughed easily. "The Dogon do not yet understand that the best hunters are not men with angry expressions, but the small beasts of many legs, who weave beautiful nets to capture their prey without effort. The spider is truly the king of beasts, but the Dogon are still too young a race to understand.''

"Aren't you one of them?" Remo asked.

The dwarf took Remo's measure with kindly eyes. "Do I appear to be one of them?"

Remo had to laugh. "No, I guess not." The dwarf slapped him on the back like an old friend. What a strange character this little squirt is, Remo thought. "Where do you come from, then?"

"I am of the Tellem tribe."

"Oh." Remo had never heard of the Tellem before. But then, he realized, he hadn't known or cared very much about the world outside of his work before the Master's Trial. "Are your people nearby?"

The dwarf squinted, surveying the ragged cliffs on all sides of them. "We are everywhere," he said. "The Tellem are an ancient race, older than time. We believe that the first men on earth were of our tribe. The spirits of those first men have stayed within us."

"And you live . . ."

"In the caves. In the hills. On the grass plains. The Tellem keep no home. We are like the spider—small, almost invisible, who can weave her nets anywhere. Yet she finds the prey she seeks because her net accepts all, watches everything, discards no being because of its appearance."

Remo looked at him for a long moment. There was no need to ask the dwarf's name. He reached into his pocket and produced the piece of carved jade.

The dwarf matched it with his own. "Kiree," he said.

"Remo."

"We will go to the cliffs."

"Kiree—" Remo took the dwarf's arm.

"You do not wish to fight?"

"No. I don't like to fight men who aren't my enemies."

"Ah," Kiree said. "I thought you did not possess the face of one who kills for pleasure."

"Then—"

"The choice is not ours, my friend. We fight not out of hatred for each other, but out of respect for the Master's Trial. For our ancestors."

Remo gritted his teeth. The longer he was involved with the Master's Trial, the more he hated it. "There never seems to be any way out," he said so quietly that he could have been talking to himself.

"Do not be confused. See, the *kanaga*, the dancers, are performing the dance of death. It is a happy dance, for the spirit of the dead is about to be reborn." He squeezed Remo's shoulder. "We, too, when our time comes, will leave this world to return, stronger, wiser, better."

He took Remo away from the crowd to the base of a cliff unobstructed by houses. It was a slab of rock so sheer that an egg could have rolled down the height of it without cracking. From a leather pouch tied around his waist, Kiree poured some yellowish powder into his palms and spat, rubbing his hands together.

Remo knew better than to question the man's fighting ability. Pint-sized or not, if Chiun considered him in the same league with Ancion, Kiree had to know what he was doing. But he didn't expect the little man to climb straight up the cliff.

Remo watched in amazement. As far as he knew, no one outside of Sinanju could scale walls without tools.

"Do you need assistance?" Kiree called, his face anxious.

"No, thanks," Remo said. He began the methodical climb, using his toes and the suction of his palms to carry the momentum of his movement upward. It was an elementary move, learned during the first year of his training with Chiun, and Remo executed it perfectly. And yet Kiree was so much faster than he was that Remo felt as if he were crawling.

The African moved on all fours, his limbs bent. He even resembled the spiders he so admired, swift, agile, modest. Remo remembered the way he'd disparaged the talents of his prospective opponents in the Master's Trial. He would never underestimate anyone again, ever.

When Remo reached the high plateau, Kiree was picking large handfuls of dried grass.

"What's that?"

"My weapon," Kiree said.

"Grass?"

The dwarf rubbed the blades together until they were powder in his hands. The movements he made were so fast that even Remo couldn't see them. Kiree spat into his palms and, with a series of intricate movements, worked his fingers until the mixture was a rubbery pulp. Then he poured some of the material from the pouch around his waist into the mass and worked it in.

"This is resin from the fruit pulp of the bala tree," he said. "To make it last."

"What are you going to do with that stuff?"

Kiree smiled. "Watch."

Throwing his arms wide, the mixture spun into a rope in the air. While it was still suspended, he tossed out another. And another, weaving them skillfully into a configuration of knots and spaces. When he was finished, he held a finely woven net as translucent as gossamer.

"I can't believe what I just saw," Remo said.

"It is but a crude imitation. The spider needs no materials other than what she carries in her tiny body."

"The spider," Remo said. "If I'd listened, I would have known. Some of the people around here believe you're an insect."

"I am a Tellem. Our lives are secret, so people will think of us what they may. Shall we begin?"

Remo hesitated. "I want to learn this skill of yours, Kiree."

"But you have already. I have shown you. The teachings of Sinanju have given you hands fast enough to weave the nets."

"But we don't have to—" His feet swept out from under him. In a fraction of a second, the net had engulfed him and carried him soaring into the air.

"Defend yourself, heir of Sinanju," the African said solemnly.

Remo was whirling over the cliff edge, unbalanced and frightened. The dwarf's easy manner, his friendly smile, had led Remo to believe that somehow the battle between them would not take place. But Kiree, like Ancion, obeyed the rules of the Master's Trial. And if Remo did not, he knew, he would die.

Slashing through the fine ropes with the cutting edges of his hands, he somersaulted through the opening to land, sliding, on the face of the cliff. His hands burned and bled from the ropes. As he tried to regain his balance on the glass-sheer cliff, Kiree's net shot out, closed, and knocked him to his belly.

Remo rolled fifteen feet or more down the rock. Below, far away, the villagers stopped their dance and pointed. From somewhere, the name of "Kiree" was shouted in fear and reverence.

The net, bigger this time, came out of the sky like a cloud. Remo scrambled out of its way and grasped one of the knots. He felt himself being lifted.

The dwarf had the strength of an army, Remo thought. He let go of the net just as it reached the edge of the plateau. *An army* . . . If there were more than one of Kiree, Remo would automatically have chosen an inside line attack. It depended on leverage and speed, and was designed to take out several opponents at once.

But why not? he thought, preparing the attack. Kiree's nets went out once more, and missed. Remo was in motion, a motion so upredictable that even Kiree's net could not follow it.

Confused, the African waited, shifting his balance, trying to follow Remo with his eyes, his hands reaching out to establish the strange pattern the white man was using. By the time Remo reached him, the nets were in disarray. Kiree moved swiftly, but Remo struck. Kiree flew backward, landing hard on his spine. Remo was right behind him. But even as he was descending for the mortal attack, Remo saw the dwarf spit into his hands and pull apart a thin rope, translucent as a fishing line. It was aimed precisely at Remo's neck.

He broke his descent with an awkward motion and landed in a painful position on his leg. The dwarf was coming, the line in his hands stretched taut.

Reflexively, Remo's elbow jutted out and caught Kiree in the base of the abdomen. With a grunt, the dwarf shot upward, doubled over. Remo sprang to his feet, and on the African's descent, Remo jumped to full extension, slashing both arms in a scissor movement.

He heard the crack of the bones in Kiree's neck. The dwarf was dead before he reached the ground. As Remo stood panting, his leg and hands feeling as if they were broken into a hundred pieces, Kiree's body thudded onto the rocky plateau.

It was over. Remo clasped his own hands together tightly. "Why?" he called out in anguish, looking at the small body at his feet. "I didn't want to kill him. He didn't deserve to die."

It echoed through the empty hills. He was afraid to move.

Maybe he should never have learned the teachings of Sinanju, he thought. He wasn't worthy of it. A true Master would have found a way to stop the fight. But then, neither Ancion nor Kiree had permitted the fight to stop.

Nothing made sense. Nothing. He had spent a lifetime fighting fools and mindless killers and human vermin, and within a week he had discovered two men who could match him in every respect. And he had killed them both.

Who was the mindless killer now?

I'm supposed to kill bad guys, he thought. Not Kiree, who accepted me as his friend. Not Ancion, so fair that he allowed me to live when he could easily have finished me in a stroke.

"Father, this test is too difficult for me," he whispered. But Chiun's voice did not come. Whatever he had to learn from the Master's Trial, he had to learn alone.

He carried Kiree's body to a far cliff and buried it beneath a small bala tree. He chose the spot because there was a spider in one of the branches, spinning a net as fine as gossamer. He spoke to the spider.

"May your spirit return quickly, my friend," he said.

The spider threw out a strand of silk and added it to her net.

Chapter Eleven

Tired. So tired.

The Dutchman staggered between the two wooden posts that signaled the division between Chinese Manchuria and North Korea along the rutted road where he walked. It was dawn again, and from the dawn when he left the Russian girl in the forest to the present one, he had known nothing. The beast inside him had run wild, feasting its desires at its every whim, not sleeping, not eating. The long path he had walked was strewn with death and calamity.

Perhaps his own death was coming soon. He hoped for it, longed for it. With death would come the peace he had never known. He trudged ahead, exhausted and burning from the spent incandescence of his power. The power was a volatile thing. With each exertion, it seared his brain and body like a firebomb. Without rest, the power would surely destroy what little sanity still remained somewhere inside him. Like a burning star, the Dutchman would consume himself in his own flames.

But without death. The beast would see that he lived, tortured and agonized, until he was an old man.

By mid-afternoon, he could smell the sea. The voices of fishermen drifted toward him, their snatches of conversation complaining about the weather and the catch. The Dutchman followed the voices.

On a gravel path walked three men passing a bottle among them. One of them stumbled, hanging on to the others for support. "Look, a white," he said in provincial Korean.

"Probably a spy. There was another not long ago. I saw him on the beach."

"In the shape you're in, you'd see mermaids. With three tits." The men snorted and doubled over with laughter.

"Can you direct me to the village of Sinanju?" the Dutchman asked them in perfect Korean. The men looked surprised.

"I think it's over that way," the most coherent of them said, pointing vaguely inland.

"Thank you." The Dutchman did not turn away, but stared instead into the man's eyes. He was growing comfortable with the beast within him. It wanted to play. "That's a nasty burn on your arm."

"Hm? What?" The fisherman glanced down at his arm. "There's nothing wrong with—" He sucked in his breath. Before his eyes, the man's forearm bubbled into red, seeping blisters. "What's happened?"

The others came around to examine the arm. It was swelling to twice its size. The hair on it frizzled and disappeared. The outer skin dried, then blackened.

The man screamed. The others drew back, watching the Dutchman with alarm.

"Take out your eyes," he commanded the man holding the bottle.

With a shudder, the man squatted on the ground and broke the bottle on a rock.

"Yi Sun!" the third man said. But the eyes of the man

with the broken bottleneck in his hands never left the Dutchman. Viciously he struck his own face with the jagged glass, digging deep into his eye sockets until streams of clear liquid poured out of them and two pulpy masses hung down his cheeks.

The third man emitted a wail that was half-whisper, half-sob, and skittered backward.

"You!" the Dutchman called.

The man covered his face and ran. Within ten paces he dropped, the ground red with scattered blood and intestines for a hundred feet in all directions. His belly had exploded.

The Dutchman threw his head back and laughed. The power, coursing through him, filled him with ecstasy. Then, as quickly as the sensation had come, it vanished, leaving him groggy and weak.

He vomited. There was blood in the thin liquid that came out of him. *Not long . . . not long now.* His body was skeletal, his vision blurry.

Find Chiun. And then, his promise fulfilled, he could seek death in peace. If he accomplished his mission, Nuihc's spirit would allow him some comfort at the end. He had promised him rest.

Chiun was nearby. The caves. There was a force coming from one of them, a power, a music. He had reached his quarry.

"Thank you, Nuihc," he whispered, stumbling forward blindly.

Rest. After a lifetime of torment, he would find rest at last.

The tiny porcelain cup in H'si T'ang's hands dropped to the floor.

"Master?" Chiun asked, moving to the old man's side. "Are you not well?"

"He is here." He gestured with a trembling hand toward the opening of the cave. "The Other . . . the Other has come."

Chiun sprang to his feet and waited in the shadows of the cave entrance.

"But something is wrong. His aura is broken, almost disappeared. . . . Now, my son. Now."

Chiun prepared to strike. There was a thud outside, then silence.

"Gone," H'si T'ang said, confused. "The presence is gone."

Chiun peered out. Lying in front of the entranceway was the emaciated form of a man with blond hair, his face in the dirt. He was barely breathing.

"It is a wounded man," Chiun said. He lifted the body gently over his shoulder and carried him inside. "Whoever he is, he will not harm us now." He lowered the man onto the grass mat.

And gasped.

"What is it, my son?"

"I know this man," Chiun said. "He is the protegee of Nuihc."

"Ah, Nuihc. I might have known." The old man trembled. The story of Nuihc was well known to him. The pupil who had used his knowledge to betray his village to the Chinese army. Who had offered to exploit the teachings of Sinanju to further his own personal power. The gifted student whom Chiun was forced to expel from the village and leave the Master of Sinanju with no heir for the legacy that had been passed down for a thousand years.

"He is called the Dutchman," Chiun said. "Remo and I encountered him when he was still a youth. Even though he was not yet fully developed in his training, he showed formidable powers."

He grasped the unconscious man's face and turned it toward his own. The Dutchman's mouth was still smeared with dried blood. "A boy of great promise, perverted by Nuihc into a monster. I thought he had died. I hoped, for his sake, that he had." He put his hands around the thin neck. "He is near death now. I will finish him quickly."

"Hold." H'si T'ang's voice was low and angry. "Has your experience in the outside world made you discard all the laws of your village?"

"But you yourself called him the Other."

"That does not matter. The most ancient law of Sinanju forbids a Master from killing a member of the village. Or have you conveniently forgotten your crime?"

Chiun swallowed. "He is not of the village. He is white."

"Was Nuihc?"

Chiun hung his head.

"I heard of your action in the battle against Nuihc. It shamed me. It shamed the gods. Now, this man is Nuihc's heir. The gods have sent him to you as your atonement."

"Teacher, I had no choice in the death of Nuihc. Without my intervention, he would have killed my son, who was too young to defend himself against him."

H'si T'ang was silent. "Your son," he said at last. "Your son Remo must fight this man. Not you."

"But Remo is so far. He will not return for many weeks. And this man is a danger to us."

'He is your penance. The ancient laws are strict. This man has come to replace Nuihc. If you kill him, you will never find peace. In this world or the next."

"But the Dutchman will try to destroy us, Master. I know him."

"Then so be it," the old man said.

Chiun sat staring at his teacher for some time as the Dutchman lay unconscious beside them. He had done what was necessary, but perhaps H'si T'ang was right. For the circle of fate to be complete, he had to be punished. He would have to face the Dutchman, alive, without killing him.

If only Remo knew what he really was! The Dutchman had been aware since childhood of his own extraordinary nature, but Remo still thought of himself as an ex-policeman. Until Remo understood that he was Shiva, a being not of this world, there would be no contest between them. The Dutchman, full grown now, developed to the pinnacle of his capabilities, would swat Remo, like a fly, into the Void.

Reluctantly, Chiun took a damp cloth and attended to the Dutchman.

Chapter Twelve

He called her Mildred and she called him Harry. He told
her he would take care of all her calls. She told him some
she would rather do herself. He said every moment she
wasted doing menial chores, grass died on this earth.
Maybe by the millions of blades.

Mildred Pensoitte thought that was very perceptive, but
she still felt more effective doing some things herself. She
felt she never wanted to lose her sense of humanity by
delegating everything to others. She should never forget,
she said, that she was just part of the whole earth. She
didn't want to be like those ruining the world. If dear, dear
Harry could understand this, her power came from understanding her place on the earth, in the earth and of it. And
the minute she lost that sense and realization, they were all
lost.

Harold W. Smith nodded and said somberly that he
understood. Then he bribed the switchboard operator to let
him listen in on all Dr. Pensoitte's calls. He listed in on a
call from Leeds, England, her mother mentioning that she
had seen Mildred's former husband the other day. A lovely
man.

"Anything else, Mother?" asked Dr. Pensoitte.

"We saw you on the telly."

"Which speech? The one for the new world order or the one on how we are poisoning ourselves?"

"One of them, dear. You were wearing that full blouse again. Do you really think that they do that much for you?"

It all might have been funny, Smith thought, if he hadn't seen a chambermaid with her throat opened to the air. That would be just the first death of many if these people were allowed to grow. Because to save the world from man, they would have to kill men, many of them, and keep killing until everyone left agreed with their vision.

Hitler had had his superior race; these people had their superior morality. Smith had to tell himself this while listening to Mildred talk to her mother, because she was so very beautiful. And she had the sort of elegant charm few women could manifest. It didn't come with smooth little-girl faces or unwrinkled bodies. It had to be tempered with time and will and the force of the person coming through, with the baby-fat of the soul removed.

Later that night, Smith checked his computers and found that the killer group had moved. It had been in Virginia and then North Carolina, and now the computer read: "Suspect penetration, St. Martin's, French Antilles. Hold target until penetration source identified."

The message gave Smith a chill, because it was a message that had been captured from the would-be presidential assassins. It showed that they knew their operation was being monitored by computers on St. Martin's. And that was where CURE's backup computers had been placed by Smith.

The killer organization was obviously computer-run to have been able to learn that. And Mildred Pensoitte's organization hadn't even had a computer until he had introduced one to help make the very wealthy Earth Goodness, Inc. into a little poverty-stricken club. Were the killers using Earth Goodness for a cover?

It didn't matter. As long as they had to deal with CURE's auxiliary computers on St. Martin's, they would delay the hit on the president. But at least now he had a shot at them. He knew where they would be. And they didn't know he would be there.

"I'll be back in a few days, Mildred," Smith told his new employer the next morning. "Personal matter."

"Will we be all right, Harry?" she asked. "I feel Earth Goodness can't live without you now."

"I'll be back, Mildred," he said. He noticed how brown her eyes were. How white her neck. How elegant her smile.

The woman in France had been beautiful too, but she had been responsible for fifteen of her countrymen being tortured to death. She would have, if she could have, gotten Smith and his whole OSS group killed that day.

Dr. Mildred Pensoitte gave Smith a polite kiss on the cheek and clenched his hand in friendship.

"I hope everything works out well for you, Harry," she said.

"I'm sure it will," he answered, reminding himself that he was married to Irma, loved Irma, and was not about to alter a lifetime of rectitude for a beautiful smile.

St. Martin's was hot under the Caribbean sun. Tourists divested themselves of their northern clothes and opened their collars and sighed while waiting on line at the airport.

Harold W. Smith wore a gray three-piece suit and kept his tie perfectly knotted. He did not perspire, and when he reached customs, he showed them his international clearance to be carrying a pistol. He did not perspire in the back seat of the taxi, which drove him past the beach at

Bay Rouge. At least two persons a year died in the apparently harmless surf there, that beautiful long white sand
beach with its softly rolling, apparently gentle surf.

But the beach dropped off at a strong enough angle that
if someone got caught in the strong Caribbean undertow,
with the surf coming in atop them, they could be rolled
around senseless, knocked off their feet by the surf rolling
back along the angle of of the beach, and made weak and
helpless in sight of people on the beach, people who had
been known to look at others crying for help and go back
to looking for seashells because to walk out into that surf
themselves might get them killed.

Smith had long ago stopped wondering what sort of
person could live with himself, watching another person
drown.

St. Martin's, of course, did not advertise the fact of its
dangerous beach because one did not want to frighten
tourists. After all, the Bay Rouge beach claimed only two
lives a year, and besides, there was an even more dangerous beach on the island. Neither of them had warnings
posted.

Like the beach, St. Martin's was deceptive, and it was
no accident that the auxiliary computers of CURE had
been planted there on the French side of the half-French,
half-Dutch island.

The computer site could be defended easily, not only by
Remo and Chiun, but by Smith himself. And the local
gendarmerie was not concerned at all about what went on
along the road to the cul de sac near Mark's Place, the
restaurant set off the main road on the way to a gentle little
harbor from which tourists set out to Pine Island to snorkel
in the Lucite-clear waters.

Off the road in what appeared to be a gravel works was
CURE's duplicate set of computers. Every day trucks
hauled gravel in and another crew hauled the same gravel

out, and everyone kept quiet about this madness lest the crazy white man who paid for this get wise to the fruitlessness of the project.

From time to time, bodies had appeared nearby, and the gendarmerie had not been concerned. They were not concerned because of a French government policy that dictated that gendarmes be moved around from island to island periodically so that they would not become native and become relaxed.

But the policy failed to realize that the police regarded the Caribbean as pre-retirement duty, and had as little interest in getting involved or in preventing crime as the average New York City subway rider.

If one was going to be transferred shortly to another island, these gendarmes thought, the one thing not wanted was to get involved in a lengthy police case or court trial on a previous island.

St. Martin's was perfect for the computers, which were deceptively vulnerable. All a person had to do to find them was to look for the extra electrical lines because in the Caribbean computers needed to be constantly air-conditioned to prevent malfunctions. The electrical lines were as easy to follow as a roadmap. From the gravel works, the lines went over the road past the small secondary airport of the island, running above a salt flat now gone to marsh, directly into the side of the mountain.

Also stored nearby were drums of oil to run the backup generators, should the overhead power fail.

And what it all said to anyone who was looking for such a direction was: "Here it is."

Even more convenient was the unlocked gate that looked like a small storage area in the side of the mountain. There weren't even guards at night.

So three men found it easily and waited for night, then took a few pounds of cordite to eliminate whatever looked like the most vulnerable parts of a computer. They entered through the unlocked gate, almost whistling with the casualness of it all.

All three saw the flash of the gun because light traveled faster than sound. But one of them did not hear the sound because a bullet reached his brain before his eardrums could send the message there.

Harold W. Smith had fired his gun again.

He shot again at the first fast movement of the two remaining. The slug hit one chest-center, dropping him. The last man threw up his hands in surrender.

The unlocked gate had led to a perfect blind ambush.

One man lay dead on the floor, the other dying, his heart pumping up a little fountain of blood, and Smith pointed his gun at the last one.

"You speak English?"

"Shit, yes. Don't shoot. For God's sakes, don't shoot."

"Who are you? What are you doing here?"

"I'm just following orders."

"Whose orders?" Smith asked.

"Theirs."

"Who ordered them?"

"I don't know."

"Think," Smith suggested.

"I don't know."

Smith heard the terror in the voice. He did not like this dirty work. He did not like to see men afraid of him or dying, but he had spent much of his life doing things that he did not like, things that he knew he had to do.

He made an obvious motion of cocking the old pistol.

"With me," he said, "You're dead now. With your bosses back in the States, maybe you'll get lucky and live."

"We just get orders."

"From whom?"

"Our leader. That's all. She phones."

"Dr. Pensoitte?" Smith asked.

"I don't know. Just a woman's voice."

"Are you paid or what?"

"No. Not paid. Money is evil. You can't be paid for being part of the earth. I don't want to die, mister."

"Neither does the president, but you men have tried twice to kill him."

"We follow orders," the youth said.

"How did you infiltrate the Secret Service?"

"I don't know what you mean," the man said.

"Why doesn't the Secret Service act when its computers pick up threats against the president?" Smith repeated.

"Oh," the young man said, his tone indicating he had an answer and thought he might use it to bargain with. Smith's steely gaze changed his mind. The man pointed to one of his dead companions. "Him, I guess. He was with the Secret Service, working with their computer system. He must have been able to jigger it up so it could ignore warnings or stuff."

"Where is your group based?" Smith asked.

"The whole world's our home."

"Where did you get your training?" Smith asked.

"All over."

"Give me an address."

"Marigot," said the young man, and Smith knew it was the main French city on the island. "I live here."

Smith waved his pistol at the two other men. "Did they live here too?"

"No. They flew down for this job. I live with my father."

"Is he part of it too?"

"No. He thinks we're crazy."

"You're very close to death, son. What do you think?"

"I think I'm scared," said the young man.

"Get the bodies outside," Smith said.

Both were dead now, heads flopping, banging harmlessly on the volcanic rock floor of the entrance to the small cave. Smith helped move the bodies and realized what he was doing. He was encouraging the young man to make a run at him so he could shoot him quickly, so he didn't have to look at the terror and shoot its eyes out.

He realized he had always hated killing. It was easier to die, he thought, than to kill. The dead mind nothing. But he had no right to die now; he had no right to risk his life. There was a country he had to protect.

When the two bodies were out into the salt marshes, the young man said, "Okay?"

"Yes," Smith said.

The young man had a condominium just outside Marigot, the French capital city. It overlooked a stretch of pure sea water facing the very flat island of Anguilla. The sun set behind that island.

The apartment looked like a library for Earth Goodness, Inc. There was a tract on why democracy was evil. The title was "When the Grass Votes, then We'll Vote."

"What phone do you get your orders on?" Smith said. He knew St. Martin's communications system was primitive, and there might be a radio hookup to the telephone that he could trace.

The boy shrugged.

"The phone," Smith repeated. "They called you, you said."

"Well, kind of," said the young man, and his eyes flashed for just an instant. Smith whirled and fired at the same time. A large blond hulk of a man was lunging at him with a lead pipe. And all the training Smith had believed was gone with time came back in an instant. The shot entered the man's chest, and he fell forward, knocking Smith to the floor, dying on top of the CURE director, but Smith held onto the gun.

And from the floor, he pointed it up at the other young man's groin.

"Good-bye," he said. He cocked the revolver.

"The Earth Goodness Society, Inc.," the young man said. "It's at 115 Pismo Beach Drive, Minneapolis, Minnesota. Mizz Robin Feldmar, student advisor. I was one of her students at Du Lac College. So were those other two guys. Him too. That one on you. She always called me. I stay here with my dad."

"As I said," Smith repeated. "Good-bye."

He fired one shot and sent Daddy's little bundle of presidential assassin off on his first leg to an expensive cemetery somewhere in America.

By dawn, Smith was on a first-class Eastern flight out of Julianna Airport on the Dutch side of the island, heading toward Minneapolis. If he could find the link between Dr. Pensoitte and that student advisor, he could work down from the top and end it all.

Did he want to find that link though?

He was an old man, and he was tired and he didn't care. He had killed again, and the death was on him, even though he had left his bloodied jacket and shirt back in St. Martin's. He flew first-class so that he could sleep, but he didn't sleep.

Back in St. Martin's, the French police reported an amazing four suicides in different parts of the island, two just outside Grand Case near the gravel works, and two in Marigot. All four suicides used the same gun, which was not found.

Chapter Thirteen

After the dusty cliffs of Mali, London was like another planet. A welcome planet, Remo decided, in a friendly galaxy where everyone spoke English.

He'd managed to make it off the African continent in one piece and, thanks to a three-day stint breaking stallions in Morocco, even had enough money in his pocket for dinner and a bed in a half-star hotel.

It had been more than two weeks since he'd left Sinanju. Two tough, sad, mixed-up weeks. God only knew how much longer the Master's Trial would take. How much of it he *could* take. He had wrestled with thoughts of life and death and honor every waking moment for the past two weeks. He was tired. He needed a rest from his own thoughts.

He wasn't going to leave for the wilds of Wales until morning. So, he decided, for tonight he wouldn't think. Not about Ancion, or Kiree, or what was to come. For tonight, he would give himself a celebration of soap and water and a clean bed and dinner in the Cafe Royal.

It was obviously a waste of money to have dinner in one

of London's best restaurants, since Remo's digestive system couldn't handle anything but rice and fish and water, but he didn't care. This was his night. He duked the headwaiter five pounds and got the best table in the place, with squishy red leather banquettes to sit on and real English roses to look at beneath the painted Edwardian ceiling. A perfect table.

Except that it was a table for two, and there was only one of him.

"Well, what did you expect?" he asked himself. "You don't know anyone here. You don't know anyone anywhere. You want to be surrounded by friends, kid, you're in the wrong profession."

He guessed he was, but there wasn't anything he could do about it. Loneliness was part and parcel of the life that had been foisted on him. He had dreamed, once, of finding a woman and making a normal life for himself. His fantasies included every corny cliché he could imagine, from kids in the rumpus room to a white picket fence. With time, though, he grew to realize that even such an ordinary ambition would be impossible for him.

He was different. His very body was different. His nervous system was more complex than other men's, the result of years of exercises on his senses. His digestive processes had simplified to the point where he could no longer ingest meat or alcohol, relegating him to a constant diet of unappetizing foods. The training of Sinanju had made him one of the best assassins who had ever lived, but it had also deprived him of any possibility of ever connecting with another human being.

He sipped his water and watched the other diners, romantic couples and merry groups.

Only one person came in unattended. Not for long, Remo guessed. There had to be some guy with a fat cigar and a fatter bankroll waiting for her. She was easily the most beautiful woman in the room. Her gold-blonde hair was pulled back into an elegant knot at the nape of her neck, setting off the classic, poetry-and-polo features of her face. She wore a white dress with a little cape of sheer stuff around her shoulders. Probably owns a castle somewhere, Remo thought. The Lady Griselda, raised on horseback and weaned on high tea.

The woman's eye caught his own. Involuntarily Remo smiled. She stopped where she stood, leaving the headwaiter to wend his way halfway around the room before noticing that he'd lost her. She took in Remo with a deep, studious glance. It wasn't sexual, just curious, as if Remo were an interesting exhibit in a museum.

"I'd like to sit over there," she told the impatient waiter. With a curt nod, he led her in Remo's direction.

"Hello, Remo," she said, kissing him lightly on the cheek.

She had the most compelling eyes he'd ever seen. They were light, but beyond that, he couldn't decide on their color. The irises seemed to shift from gray to pale blue to turquoise to yellow-green and deep emerald, with a hundred shades in between.

"It's so nice to see you. Do you mind if I join you?"

She spoke with a slight accent. So she wasn't English, after all. And she knew Remo's name. He racked his brains trying to remember who she was, but nothing registered.

"Uh—I'd be delighted," he said, rising.

No, he didn't know her, he decided. There was no way he could have forgotten those eyes.

When the waiter had gone, she said, "I hope you don't mind my barging in on you like this. I hate to dine alone. Don't you?"

And a mind-reader, too, he thought. "I've gotten used to it."

"Yes," she said appreciatively. "I imagine you have."

The wine steward came over with a list. Remo asked the woman if she felt like something to drink, hoping she knew enough about wine to make her own selection. It had been so long since Remo had touched alcohol that he'd forgotten the names on the labels.

"I'll have vodka," the woman said.

The waiter nodded. "A martini?"

"A bottle. And a water glass."

The unflappable waiter left. Remo smiled. "We've never met," he said.

"No."

"How did you know my name?"

"I guessed."

What kind of a con is this, he thought. "What's yours?"

"What would you like it to be?"

He sighed. A call girl. "I've got fifty-two dollars," he said flatly. "That's it."

"Good for you."

He was embarrassed. "I only meant—"

The waiter showed up with the vodka and a large tumbler, which he filled to the brim.

"Have you decided on a name for me yet?" she asked, raising her glass.

"How about Sam?" he asked drily. "I knew a guy named Sam once who drank vodka by the bucket."

"Sam it is, then." She downed the glass in one draught.

"Who are you?" Remo asked.

"I thought we just decided on that."

"Come off it. My guess is you're some kind of bored society dame acting cute with the hoi-polloi—"

She laughed. "Not at all. I'm new in London. I walked in here alone, saw you, and sat down. Does everything have to be so complicated?"

"Have it your way," Remo said. "Are you hungry?"

"Starving."

"Figures." He eyed the prices on the menu. His fifty-two dollars might stretch as far as one meal and two bottles, all for her. Another breakfast of berries along the side of the road.

"I'd like fish," she said. "Raw."

He sat still for a moment, then leaned over toward her. "How much do you know about me?"

"Why should I know anything about you? Are you famous?"

"The fish."

"It's much better raw. You ought to try it."

Well, maybe it was just a coincidence, he said to himself. He sat back, trying frantically to remember where he might have met her before. It was useless. "All right," he said.

The waiter set down their platter of raw fish at arm's length, regarding his two customers as if he expected them to jump wildly onto the tables at any moment.

The woman sent him away with a haughty stare. She picked up a sliver of fish with her fingers and slid it delicately into her mouth.

"Do you have something against silverware?" Remo asked.

"Useless," she said, offering a piece to Remo. Her nails were short and unpainted. She wore no makeup. And those eyes of hers were driving Remo crazy.

"What color are they?" he blurted.

"My eyes?" She shrugged. "Blue. Gray. Green. They change."

"Really strange," he muttered.

"How flattering. You've encountered your share of strange people, I suppose?"

"You have no idea."

"I think I do." She downed another tumbler of vodka.

"Get some rice for yourself. That's what you eat, isn't it?"

He threw his napkin on the table. "Okay. Come clean. What are you doing here?"

"Calm down, Remo."

"Bulldookey!"

"Bulldookey?"

"There's no way you could have guessed my name."

"You sound like Rumplestiltskin. Eat your fish. You must be exhausted."

"I *am* exhausted. But you don't have any business knowing that."

She leaned over and kissed him full on the mouth. Stunned, he felt as if his spine had just turned into an electric eel. The temperature in the room seemed to rise to the level of a pizza oven. When their lips finally broke away, he noticed that people all over the restaurant were staring at them. "What was that for?" he asked, dazed. "Not that I minded. Maybe you'd like to try it again for practice."

"Later," she said, resuming her meal.

"Later," Remo grumbled. She was playing some kind of game, but he was too tired to figure it out. And why bother, anyway, he decided. She was nuts, end of discovery. Still, kissing her beat eating restaurant rice at a table for one any day.

"I'm staying at Claridge's. Will you come with me?"

He gulped, standing up instantly. "Twisted my arm," he said.

Inside the doorway of her darkened room, she put her arms around him. He tried to gear himself up for the fifty-two steps to ecstasy, but something was different. Her touch was warm, electrifying, comforting. There was no naughty boom-boom about this girl. Even without speaking, he felt as if he had known her all his life, this girl whose name he didn't even know.

Remo had loved many women in his time. And yet none of them had felt like this one. There was something sure about it, as if their flesh belonged together, and always had. But he was being an idiot, he told himself. Any woman who wouldn't even give her name to a man she was going to spend the night with wasn't exactly in the market for true love.

"I suppose you're being so mysterious just so you can avoid talking to me if we ever bump into each other again."

She let her arms fall from around his neck. "Your ways are too worldly for me to understand," she said simply. "I cannot tell you who I am because I cannot. That is all there is to know. And I wish to make love with you because my body longs for you. Is it not enough?"

Strange bird. Even in the darkness he could see the changing tones of her eyes. Remo kissed her gain. "It's enough," he said. And for some reason he didn't understand, going to bed with this woman seemed to be more important to him than breathing.

He made love to her like a schoolboy, frightened, delighted, surprised at his own artlessness. He forgot everything about the sexual techniques that worked with other women, because this nameless girl was like no other woman he had ever been with. They laughed together and played and wrestled and touched each other like incalculably precious things, and Remo told her stories about the orphanage where he'd grown up, and she sang him lewd Viking songs about the glories of raping and looting in the land of the Francs, and when they finally came together, it was as if he'd never made love to anyone before.

He held her close until she slept.

"Sam?"

She didn't answer. Her breathing was slow and regular.

"I think I love you," he whispered, shocked at his own words, grateful that she hadn't been awake to hear them.

Her mouth curved into a smile.

"You faker!" he muttered, pushing her away. He could feel himself blushing.

She entwined herself around him and found his lips again. "Bulldookey," she said.

Chapter Fourteen

He shook her awake. "Sam. I've got to go."

She squinted, turning toward the window. The first red streaks of dawn showed. "Where?"

"Wales," he said.

She sat up, rubbing her eyes. Her hair was still in its knot, dangling down the side of her neck. She was so pretty that Remo was half afraid to look at her. He knew that the more time he spent with her, the more he would want to stay. He got up and dressed quickly.

"Can I go with you?"

"No."

"Why not?"

"Because I say so."

"Oh." She sounded hurt.

"Hah. It hurts when the shoe's on the other foot, doesn't it?"

"What shoe?"

"It's just an American expression. What country are you from, anyway? Ah-ah-ah, just testing. I know you aren't going to tell me."

She stretched herself like a cat. The sight of her naked body in daylight gave Remo a pang of sadness. He dropped his shoe and stood for a few moments, watching her, wondering if he would ever see her again.

"Let's quit this," he said, disgusted.

"What?"

"This secrecy crap. I want us to see each other again. Tell me how I can reach you."

"I'll follow you," she said.

He shook his head. He didn't trust himself to talk.

"Why not?" she asked.

"You can't, that's all. Not where I'm going."

"Oh, I see. You think I'm too frail and delicate for your rowdy life."

"You're about as frail as a Sherman tank." He slipped on his T-shirt. It smelled of her.

She walked over to him and took his hands.

"Don't, okay?" He broke away from her, suddenly angry. "You can't go, and I can't tell you why, and this is the last time I'm going to see your funny face because, for some reason, you want us to keep on being strangers. So don't make it any harder than it already is." He walked to the door.

"Remo . . ." She came to him and kissed him. And again, it felt as if she had been with him all his life.

"Tell me who you are," he whispered. "I don't care if you're on the run from somebody, or married, or whatever. I don't even care how you know about me. I just want to be able to find you when I get back."

She gazed at him for a long time. Then, frowning, she lowered her eyes.

He waited in silence for what seemed an eternity. Finally he spoke, burning with shame. "Just asking," he said bitterly.

"Please—"

"Hey. No need to make excuses. Believe me, I don't want any strings, either. It was a swell one-night stand."

He ran down the hotel steps, hot-wired the first unguarded car he saw, and laid a strip of rubber a mile long.

"Bitch," he muttered, speeding out of the city. He was never going to get mixed up with women again. He would limit himself to tarts and dumbbells. If no tarts or dumbbells were available, he'd settle for cold showers.

What was so special about what's-her-name, anyway, he asked himself. He'd just been lonesome and horny. As a matter of fact, she was as ordinary as they came. Couldn't carry a tune in a bucket. And her nose was crooked. Didn't even know how to use a fork.

She was freaking weird, when it came right down to it. Eyes that kept changing colors, like a kaleidoscope. Muscles like a damned stevedore under that silky skin. Probably lifted weights on her lunch hour. He wouldn't be surprised if she was a dyke. Or worse. One of those Scandinavian sex-change jobs. By God, that was why she wouldn't give him her name! Call me Harry, darling. Hell, he was glad to be rid of her.

But oh, the taste of her lips.

Forget it. What was done was done. Even if it never started.

He made it to Wales in record time. Stopping at a village to buy some gas with all the money he had left, he considered buying a map of the area, but discarded the idea. Michelin didn't include places like the Valley of the Forest Primeval on its maps. He was too embarrassed even to ask directions to such a ridiculous-sounding place, even if Chiun did insist that it was the correct address.

He headed north. It seemed like the more primeval route. By the time the roads changed from stone to earth, and the rickety wooden signposts touted places like Llanfairfechan and Caernarfon as major metropolises hundreds of kilometers distant, the late afternoon mist was beginning to settle along the mossy banks where he drove. The trees were huge here, lush pines stretching to the clouds. Insects and hidden forest animals seemed to be everywhere, chattering endlessly. The air was thick and sweet.

Remo drove the car down the narrowing road, overgrown almost to invisibility by grass, until the road petered off into a footpath and then, in the distance, disappeared altogether.

"Great," Remo said out loud. "Just freaking great." He must have come fifty miles on that road. "Valley of the Forest Primeval. I've got to be out of my gourd."

He slammed the gears into reverse and backed up. "Look on the bright side," he explained to the steering wheel. "The one good thing about having a rotten day is that after a certain point it doesn't get any worse, right?"

He was looking over his shoulder when the rock smashed his windscreen.

"Wrong," he muttered, getting out of the car.

There was a rustling somewhere in the forest. He ran toward it.

Nothing. Everything was still once he reached the shadows of the pines. The chipmunks and squirrels kept up their angry chatter.

Must have been a freak accident, he decided, coming back to the road. A rock that got spun up by the tires . . .

He closed his eyes, hoping it was all a bad dream, then opened them again. No dream. All four tires were flat.

He examined one. A puncture. A very neat puncture, executed by a sharp metal instrument. The others were the same.

"I can't believe it," he said. He'd always thought of vandalism as an urban problem. But there wasn't even a road here, and his tires had been slashed by a knife. He looked around. Not a footprint.

Where did they come from? Maybe the people out here imported hoodlums, like oranges. Maybe somewhere in Llanfairfechan there was a company that brought gang members from Chicago or New York by the truckload, snarling and slashing at travelers to make sure the area didn't get overrun by tourists.

He leaned against the car and slid down to a sitting position. He hadn't seen a house for thirty miles, and he'd passed the last garage four hours ago.

Hell, what was he thinking about? He didn't have any money to pay for tires even if he found them. There was nothing he could do now except wait it out till morning and then carry on on foot.

Maybe it was for the best, he thought sleepily. He hadn't gotten much rest the night before, what with squandering his one evening of relaxation on a girl. It wouldn't hurt to catch forty winks. He closed his eyes.

Ping.

"Wazzat," he said, leaping to his feet. On the car's fender, just beside the place where his head had been, was a small dent. From the angle of the mark, its trajectory had been from above.

He looked up at the trees. "Okay, you little bastards," he yelled.

Ping.

He caught it with a slap of his hand. A pebble. And another, whizzing through his hair.

He stalked through the forest, crouching, moving so that his feet didn't disturb the leaves beneath them. About fifty yards away, he caught sight of a pair of short, skinny legs in ragged pants shinnying down the trunk of a tree. A little torso covered by a leather jerkin followed, and two arms, one of them clutching a homemade slingshot. The last part down was a tiny, dirt-smeared face, its eyes wide and alert, searching in all directions.

"Graaagh," Remo yelled, snatching the boy by the scruff of the neck.

The boy screamed and kicked, his grimy limbs dangling in midair. "Let me down, you great filthy beast."

"Look who's talking," Remo said. "They can smell you in Albuquerque."

"Fight me fair, and I'll kill you, Chinee." He looked at Remo, puzzled. "You *are* the Chinee, aren't you?"

Remo lifted him until his face was level with his own. "How Chinee do I look?"

The boy's mouth set defiantly. "Well, you musta used magic to cover yourself up, like. Swine of a yellow Chinee, I know who y'are. Set me down and fight like a man."

"Oh, jeez," Remo said. He dropped the boy, who rolled a few feet in the moss like a dirty leather ball, then righted himself, his fists high. "Go on, fight me, villain."

Remo tapped him on the stomach with one finger.

"Oof." The boy fell backward. "Lucky punch, that was. Do it again. Dare you, pig."

Remo tweaked his leg. The boy somersaulted onto his back.

"I'm not down yet, Chinee," he panted, staggering to his feet. He blew a lock of unruly black hair off his forehead.

"Look, before we continue this fight to the death, suppose you tell me why you threw that rock into my windshield and cut up my tires."

"Fool. Had to get you to stop, didn't I?" He put up his fists.

"You could have asked."

The boy snorted. "And let you run away from me like the ruddy yellow coward y'are?"

"We all have to take our chances," Remo said. "How do you think I'm going to get out of this place?"

"You're not leaving alive, if that's what you have in mind."

"Oh, that's right. I forgot. You're going to finish me off here and now."

"That's right. There's nought but one winner in the Master's Trial."

"*What*?"

"Prepare to die."

The boy lunged. Remo swept him up under his arm. Now things had really gone too far. Fighting a dwarf had been bad enough. But if Chiun expected him to murder a ten-year-old kid, he could take his traditions and shove them up the old archives.

"You've got to be kidding," he said.

"By the gods . . ." The boy was flailing for all he was worth. Remo let him wear himself out. After a long, wild bout, the boy drooped exhausted, suspended by his midsection, twitching occasionally and sniffling. "By the gods, you'll not kill my father," he squeaked.

Remo set him down.

The boy wiped his nose with his sleeve. "I *will* fight ya," he said, his tears cutting little white rivulets down his cheeks. "Just need a minute to get m'strength back."

"Sure," Remo said gently, putting his arm around the boy. He didn't resist. "Suppose you tell me who your father is."

"Emrys ap Llewellyn," he said, digging his fists into his eyes. "Son of Llewellyn. I'm Griffith. Griffith ap Emrys. Son of Emrys."

"So that's how it works."

"Who're you?"

"Remo ap nobody, I guess. I'm an orphan."

The boy nodded. "I'm half an orphan. My ma's gone. Remo don't sound like a Chinee name."

"Griffith doesn't sound like the name of a killer."

"A man's got to fight, if he's a man. That's what my da says."

"Only if he's got no choice."

"What about you? You never even met my da, and you come all this way to kill him."

"I'm not going to kill your father. I've come here to tell him that."

"You're lying."

"Cross my heart."

The boy looked hopeful for a moment. Then his frown returned.

"But you'll fight him."

"Nope. Not unless he attacks me."

The boy squirmed. "Da's a funny man," he said.

"How's that?"

"He might attack you. It's the Trial rules, you know, to fight. But he can't kill you."

"Why not?"

The boy scrutinized Remo suspiciously. "Maybe I shouldn't say. It'll be giving you unfair advantage."

Remo couldn't argue. The kid was a dirtball, but he was no dummy.

"Unless you promise not to kill him, no matter what."

"Okay. That's a deal."

"No, a real promise. With this." He produced a pocketknife.

"Exhibit A," Remo said.

"Come on, hold out your finger."

"Oh, no you don't. I can't stand the sight of blood."

"It'll just be a prick on your finger. To promise." The boy waited expectantly.

"Well, all right. But not too deep."

The boy gave him an expert stab on the end of his index finger. "Okay, now swear you won't hurt my da."

"I swear."

"Swear by all the ancient gods, by Mryddin and Cos and the Lady of the Lake—"

"All right, all right already," Remo said. "Why won't your father kill me?"

The boy leaned close to Remo's ear and whispered: "Because he's going blind."

Remo straightened up. "Are you serious?"

"It's my fault. Last year, during the Midsummer Eve Feast, I climbed up a tree and couldn't get down. I was scared, you see. I'm a weak one, really, not like the other boys. I was showing off, to prove to my da . . ." His voice trailed off in shame.

"Hey," Remo said, hoisting the boy onto his lap. "Everybody gets scared. You wouldn't be normal if you didn't."

The boy stared hard at the ground, his cheeks red. "So my da came after me," he continued softly. "I was stuck on a high branch, and it was a long way down. It wasn't so strong. When my da climbed up on it to get hold of me, the branch give way. While we was falling, he put me on top of him so's I wouldn't hit ground. His head struck a great rock. He was like as dead for a fortnight or more. I prayed to all the gods there are to make him well, and he come out of it, but his eyes ain't never been the same again. And lately they been getting worse. You see, it's my fault."

"Griffith—"

" 'Tis! And now, if he fights you, he'll die sure. Don't you see, it'll be like me killing him myself. The gods are pointing at me for being a coward that day in the tree. They're going to take my da from me, like they took my ma, and then . . . And then . . ."

"Shh," Remo said, rubbing the boy's head.

"That's why it's me that's got to fight you. If you kill me, I'll deserve it. But not my da."

"Nobody's going to kill anybody, okay? There's not going to be any fight. I gave you my promise, didn't I?"

Griffith took Remo's finger and examined it. "Your sacred promise. Witnessed in blood."

"The most sacred. Now how about taking me to your dad so we can talk things over."

Griffith eyed him worriedly. "T'was your most sacred—"

"I get it, okay?"

The boy smiled. "I'll get you a horse in the morning. They're wild in these parts, and they're better than cars. I can tame them quick."

"I'd appreciate that," Remo said.

Chapter Fifteen

The boy took Remo into a green valley in the deepest part of the forest. There, tucked beneath a cluster of massive trees, stood a cottage with a newly thatched roof. Remo had to stoop to enter through the low arched doorway.

A man was inside, sharpening a knife on an oilstone. Even though he was sitting down and his back was to the door, he was a giant of a man.

"Da?" the boy said.

Emrys turned, smiling. "Well, I thought those goblins you're always talking to had ate you right this time." His smile disappeared when he saw Remo. In the dim light of the cottage, Remo could see that the man's eyes were clouded and mottled.

"Da, it's—"

"I know who it is," he said, rising. He nodded curtly to Remo. "There's but one who'd be coming to the valley now."

"He's not a true Chinee," Griffith said hopefully. "Y'see, Remo here has promised—"

"I suppose you'll want to be starting," Emrys said, ignoring his son.

"No," Remo said quickly. "As a matter of fact—"

"You're not welcome to the hospitality of my home."

"Da, let him talk. Please."

"You hold your tongue, Griffith." He strode over to the door with large, thundering steps and threw it open. "We'll talk outside. You stay in and mind your silence." He locked the door behind him.

"Da . . ."

"I've chosen a place. You can see if it suits you," he told Remo as they walked toward a clearing in the glen.

Remo could hear the boy's voice calling frantically from inside the cottage. "You promised, Remo! Don't forget your promise. T'was made in blood!"

The big man removed the sheepskin vest he wore and draped it neatly over a rock. From inside the hollow of an oak he took a piece of bark covered with strange words. "A message for my son," he said, laying the scrap of wood on top of the vest. From his trousers pocket, he extracted the carved jade stone Chiun had given him and threw it at Remo's feet. "There's the rock. It's begun now."

Remo breathed deeply. "Emrys, I'm not going to fight you."

The man's mouth turned down into a bitter scowl. "What's Griffith been telling you?"

"That you have no more reason to go through with this farce than I do," Remo said. "Tradition or not, I've seen enough of the Master's Trial to know it's a crock. Let's end it here and now. For everybody's sake." He extended his hand.

Emrys shoved past him. "I won't have it," he growled. "If you don't have the guts to fight me in the Master's Trial, then fight me as a man."

"What difference would that make?"

Emrys stared at him, his nostrils distended. "I might let you live," he said menacingly.

"Forget it. I've promised not to fight you."

"A promise to a babe."

"Who's got more sense than his father."

"Fight, damn you!"

"You'd *lose,* can't you see that?" Remo shouted. "You'd lose to a man half your size, let alone me. How far gone are your eyes? Just a little blurriness around the edges, or are shapes all you can make out?"

"Make your move, you spineless coward!"

"No. I said I wouldn't fight."

Emrys's face was contorted into a mask of rage and shame. "Then you'll die. I'll not be pitied by you."

He lunged for Remo and swung wildly, missing him by a foot. The missed blow sent him sprawling on the ground.

"Now look here," Remo said, going over to him and touching his shoulder. Just as he was about to speak, Emrys took him by surprise with a powerful roundhouse right to the jaw. Remo felt as if all his teeth had jarred loose at once.

"Who's blurry around the edges now, chopstick pecker?" He laughed, a big, hearty guffaw filled with pride.

Remo rubbed his jaw. "Very funny."

"Where'd you learn to fight, anyway, some Chinee opium den?"

Remo rolled his eyes. "My training comes from Sinanju. That's in Korea, peabrain. Not China."

He attacked. Remo ducked. "Son of a yellow whore."

"Oh, come off it."

"So that's how you fight over in Sin and Goo. With your mouth," Emrys taunted. "It's a big one, too. To make up for your lack of balls, I'll wager." He came at

Remo in a flying tackle, clutching Remo's legs with a viselike grip.

"Hey—"

Emrys flipped him over and jabbed two knuckles at his eyeballs. Before they struck, Remo took hold of the big man's arms and threw him.

"That's more like it, dogmeat," Emrys said, grinning. He leaped at Remo. Remo caught him, and the two of them wrestled, unyielding, until they were both slathered in sweat.

Remo's wrists were aching. They'd been grappling, stuck to each other like Siamese twins, for twenty minutes or more. He should have known better than to underestimate Emrys, he realized. His opponent's eyes might be failing, but he was strong as a bull.

"I know . . . how you got here," Emrys grunted.

"Ng," Remo said.

"Your . . . friend . . . Chiun . . ."

"Yeah?" He shook a bead of sweat off his nose. "What about him?"

"He shits white boys like you for turds."

Remo laughed. "You've got to be the grossest—"

Emrys used the opportunity to slam Remo in the belly, shooting him across the glen into a tree trunk.

Feeling his lungs collapse, Remo rolled out of the way of Emrys's oncoming body.

"Sorry, Griffith, but all bets are off," he mumbled, striking out with a left hook. It sliced the Welshman across the shoulder. With a howl, Emrys came at him again, throwing him into the center of the clearing like a sack of bricks.

Remo closed his eyes as he landed, grateful that Chiun wasn't around to see him fighting like a barroom brawler with a half-blind lunatic. And losing.

"This is it," Remo said, stumbling to his feet. "I'm beginning to lose patience with you."

"Arggh," Emrys gurgled, staggering forward, his fists weaving in front of him. Remo stepped out of the way. Emrys tripped on a rock and fell face down with a thud.

"You're the one who wanted to fight," Remo said, trying to focus.

"So I do." The Welshman charged.

Remo charged.

And they both fell down.

"What was that?" Remo said, cranking himself upward into a sitting position.

Emrys brushed some dust off his bare chest. "I na ken it. Summat struck me fierce upon the head. And just when I was about to finish you off, too."

"Finish *me* off?" Remo objected. "That's a—wait a second." He crawled a few feet and retrieved a long slender pole tipped by an iron arrow wound around the stick by a strip of leather. "It's a spear. I think."

Emrys searched himself for wounds. "Am I hit?"

"No. Neither am I. But it knocked both of us off our feet."

"Oh, na," Emrys moaned, his voice quavering. "We done something wrong."

"Like what?" Remo said irritably. "What are you talking about?"

Emrys pointed. "A great white form yonder. 'Tis the gods, come to seek vengeance."

Remo looked in the direction where Emrys was pointing. Through the foliage of the forest, he could make out the shape of a white horse.

"I should have listened to Griffith," Emrys said, his voice filled with doom and wonder. "He talks to the wood spirits. I never believed they was for true, but the boy knew. Now it's too late."

"It's only a horse, for crying out loud. Get yourself a pair of glasses."

"A horse that throws spears?"

Remo fingered the iron-tipped pole uncertainly "Somebody's standing behind the horse."

"You great Chinee lummox. You're blinder'n I am."

The horse galloped into the clearing, then slowed to a halt some fifty yards from the two men. The rider was a woman. She dismounted, the flowing robes she wore billowing gracefully. When she was on her feet, she gave the animal a sharp slap on the rump and sent him galloping into the wood. Then she walked forward purposefully toward the two men.

Remo looked, shook his head, looked again. "It can't be," he said slowly.

"Oh, gar," Emrys lamented.

She was the same woman Remo had spent the night with in London, but radically different. She was dressed in a loose gown of sea green, fastened at her shoulders by two large gold medallions. In her belt were a small ax and a knife. Her golden hair hung to below her waist and moved like water with each step she took. As she drew nearer, the sun caught the thin gold circlet around her forehead, making her look like a barbarian princess. Her eyes, green and gray and blue, regarded him somberly. She did not speak.

"It's you," Remo said.

She picked up the spear. Without a word, she hurled it into the forest and followed it.

"Is she real?" Emrys whispered, afraid to turn his head.

"Yeah," Remo said, then thought better of it. "Maybe."

She returned with the still warm carcass of a rabbit, a red wound where its eye had been. Silently she offered it to Emrys.

The Welshman accepted it, swallowing hard. "Well, I

suppose we could all do with a little dinner,'' he same lamely. He cleared his throat.

She turned to Remo, her head held high.

''Sam.'' He said it so softly it was almost a sigh.

''I am Jilda of Lakluun,'' the woman said. ''Here for the Master's Trial.'' Then, slowly, the strange eyes twinkling, she inclined her head to Remo in a formal bow.

Chapter Sixteen

"I prayed," Griffith said, staring into the hearth. The cottage was filled with the warm, smoky aroma of the rabbit cooking over the open fire.

Roasting meat was not one of Remo's favorite smells, but he'd learned through the years to hold his tongue in a world full of carnivores. He stayed near the window and tried to breathe shallowly.

"I asked Mryddin and all the ancient gods and the spirits to bring you both back safe, and they did. The Lady of the Lake herself brought you home. And a good fat hare, too."

"Uh," Remo said, feeling nauseated. He leaned out the window. Outside, Jilda was stalking the forest, spear in hand. "The High Executioner of the animal kingdom, you mean."

Griffith gasped. "Remo, take it back, quick. What you said was a sacrilege."

"Don't be bossing our guest, boy," Emrys said. To Remo's dismay, he was nailing the rabbit skin up to dry on the cottage wall. "Jilda's no spirit. She's a friend of Remo's."

"But she *is*! 'Tis the Lady of the Lake."

"Griffith!"

The boy crouched. "Yes, Da."

"Leave us now." Griffith slinked outside. "He holds to the old religion more than most," Emrys explained. "Sometimes I worry about him. Too much like his ma, all air and dreams. I don't know how I'll get him ready."

"For what?" Remo said.

Emrys put down his hammer and stepped back to admire the bloody pelt on the wall. "Why, for his turn at the Master's Trial, don't you know."

"What? I thought that was all over."

Emrys looked surprised. "Between us? How could it be over? I like you, Remo. Don't get me wrong now. But both of us are still alive. That's against the rules."

"Nei skynugur," Jilda muttered, bursting into the room with another rabbit hanging limply between her fingers.

"What's that you say, missy?"

"It is a Norse expression describing what I feel about the precious Master's Trial. Translated, it means 'bull-dookey.' "

She cleaned the rabbit expertly, tossing the intestines out the window, inches from Remo's face.

"Do you mind?" he said testily.

"Mind what?" Jilda asked.

Remo prepared himself for an explanation of the social unacceptability of slapping one's associates with animal organs, then waved the idea away. Even the most rudimentary forms of etiquette would be wasted on Jilda. He winced as she pulled off the rabbit's skin with a jerk and tossed it to Emrys, who nailed it happily to the wall.

"The Trial was originally begun so that our people would not make war on one another," she said. "I believe that was because someone thought that one day we might all need to band together."

"Live with a bunch of bloodthirsty Vikings?" Emrys said, genuinely surprised.

Jilda's dagger was out of her belt in a flash.

"Whoa," Remo said. "No murders till after dinner, okay?"

Jilda replaced the knife scornfully. "Anyway, I was saying we ought to be friends."

"Great start you've made," Remo said.

"But abolishing the Trial," Emrys protested.

Jilda thrust the rabbit onto the spit over the fire. "It's a stupid tradition. Maybe it served a purpose a thousand years ago, but it's time we ended it. I have given this thought, and I, for one, will not kill strangers who have done me and my people no harm."

"Bingo," Remo said. "I've reached the same decision."

"But my father was killed by the great Chinee," Emrys said.

Jilda cut him off. "So was mine. That doesn't change anything."

"Well, I don't know. I'll not be called a coward."

"Don't you see?" Jilda said, waving Griffith inside. "If all three of us refuse to fight, it won't be a question of cowardice. And your boy will be spared from having to do battle."

Emrys jutted out his chin. "You talk like you think Griffith would lose."

Griffith walked in, laughing lightly. His hands were cupped. He opened them to reveal a tiny green tree frog, which bounded out the window to the boy's cries of joy.

"Well, look at him," Jilda said, obviously annoyed. "He's a kind and clever boy, but even you can't think he'd make a decent warrior."

"I'll not have you speaking that way in my house, missy."

"That's all right," Griffith said gently. "She's right."

"You keep your peace."

"But I'm not a good fighter. I'll never be. I'm small, and my hands aren't fast."

Emrys threw down his hammer with a crash. "By Mryddin, I never thought I'd live to see a member of my family call himself a coward."

"Hey," Remo objected. "He's not a coward. He was willing to take me on himself to keep me from fighting you. That might be what you call a coward, but I'd rather have one guy like him on my side, alive, than a hundred terrific fighters who've gone to their reward during this asinine Master's Trial."

Emrys deliberated, his glance shifting from Jilda and Remo to the boy. Finally he said, "Well, I suppose you're right. Seeing as how we're about to share a meal together, there's not much reason to fight."

"Oh, Da," the boy said, hugging him.

Jilda nodded. "Then it's settled," she said. "Now we eat."

Remo sat a little apart from the others, contenting himself with a bowl of roots and wild grasses from the forest while they stabbed hungrily at the roast rabbits.

"Will you not have any?" Griffith asked.

Remo shook his head.

"Is that part of being a Chinee, eating no meat?"

"Sort of."

Jilda laughed, her eyes changing from blue to bright green. "Don't ask the Chinese to claim our Remo. He's an American. But his soul belongs with us."

Remo spoke to the dancing green eyes. "I feel as if I do belong with you . . . all," he added, flustered.

"We know," Emrys said.

Remo felt sleepy. The warm cabin, the safety of the woods . . . It all seemed so homey, and yet in the same room with him were a man who could hold him in a hammerlock for half an hour and a woman who could drop two men with the broadside of a spear.

He smiled lazily as he watched Jilda eat. The sight of her tearing off the pale meat with her fingers filled him with strange passion. She was at the same time a lady and a wild animal, beautiful and free. And he wanted her more than he had ever wanted a woman.

"You look content, my friend," Emrys said. "Although how a man can be satisfied with birds' food I'll never know."

Remo set down his bowl, making an effort to tear his gaze away from Jilda. "I am," he said. "It's funny. I feel like I'm with my own kind. I always thought Chiun and I were the only ones like us."

"And so you are," Emrys said. "What the three of us have in common is that none of us belong to the world." He took in at once the unspoken intimacy between Remo and Jilda. "But we can never be part of one another's lives without giving up our own ways. That would be worse than death. For me, at least."

Remo fought down a sudden, irrational feeling of annoyance toward the Welshman. The moment had been perfect. No questions, no thought of the future. And now Emrys had voiced a possibility Remo hadn't wanted to face: *What will I have to give up to keep Jilda with me?*

"Will you be going back to Sinanju?"

"Sinanju?" Since he'd found Jilda, he hadn't given a thought to Sinanju.

"To tell Chiun what we've done with the Master's Trial," Emrys continued. "I don't think he'll be happy with the news."

"No," Remo said. "I guess not."

"What I'm saying is, I'll go with you."

"Me, too," Griffith said. "I've yearned so to see the wild Chinee."

"You'll be staying right here, and no argument. What do you say we go tomorrow, Remo? A partner will lighten the load on your journey."

"Tomorrow . . ." Remo said. It was so soon.

Jilda stood up and went to him. "We'll all go," she said.

Remo's heart quickened. "You, too?"

"We three have made the decision, and we three will stand by it together."

"And me too, Da," Griffith pleaded, sounding desperate. "I must go with you. I'll be needed. I can feel it."

Emrys gave him a black look, and the boy subsided.

"Come," Jilda said, laying a hand on Remo's shoulder. "There's no room for us here to spend the night. We'll sleep outdoors."

"I'd planned on giving up my bed for you, miss," Emrys said kindly. " 'T'isn't often we have female visitors."

"Not necessary," Jilda said. "I am accustomed to sleeping in the open. I like to see the stars overhead."

"Same here," Remo said quickly.

The night sky seemed to shine with a million candles. In their liquid light, her long hair spread over the moss like a cape of gold, Jilda was almost terrifyingly beautiful.

Remo lay beside her, tender and spent. Their lovemaking had been even better than he'd remembered. Once again, he had felt as if he had come to her for the first time. Once again, their bodies had joined like two halves of a perfect whole.

"I'm glad you're coming to Sinanju," Remo said softly, tracing a line with his finger along the smooth, moonlit skin of her leg.

"I won't leave you until I have to."

He found it difficult to speak. "You—you don't ever have to."

"Ah, yes I will. Look. My star." She pointed to the sky. "The golden one."

It had been a dumb attempt, Remo decided. Too soon and too awkward. He'd never been good at sweet-talking women. He let it pass. "To the north?" he asked, pretending to be interested.

"Yes. Its name is Gullikona—'Golden Lady.' My parents named me for her. 'Jilda' is the name I chose for myself when I was grown."

He touched her hair. Golden Lady. Embarrassed, he pulled his hand away. He didn't want to paw her like some lovesick adolescent. What he felt was crazy. He'd have to control it.

"According to one of our legends, Gullikona was once, in the old days, a beautiful princess with hair like spun gold. Although she was betrothed to a mighty warlord, she fell in love with a young warrior and took him to her bed. When the warlord found out about her infidelity, he assigned her lover to serve on his own ship for a long voyage to distant lands. Once at sea, the warlord tortured his rival and brutally murdered him, cutting off the young man's hand. Then he sent a special messenger on a small boat to return home to present the severed hand to the princess.

"When she received the horrible present, the princess was so overcome with grief that she went to the seashore that night and built a great bonfire. Then, clasping her lover's dismembered hand between her own, she walked into the flames so that she might be with him for all time in Valhalla.

"The legend says that her burning hair made such a beautiful fire that even the gods took notice. Freya herself, goddess of love and pleasure, found pity in her heart for the doomed lovers. She plucked the princess from the earth, fire and all, and placed her in the sky, where the dead warrior's spirit would be sure to find her. And there they remain, the flames of their love burning to the end of time.''

"Gullikona," Remo whispered. "Sam—I mean Jilda—"

She laughed. "You liked Sam, didn't you? She was more refined than I am. Unfortunately, her high-heeled shoes were unbearable."

"What were you doing in London?"

"Why, looking for you, of course. I began my search in Morocco. I just missed you in Lisbon. I was afraid that you might not stop in England at all, and that I wouldn't get to meet you before my turn in the Master's Trial. But that would have been too late."

"You would have fought me?"

"I'd have had no choice. The elders of Lakluun would have been watching. That was why I had to see you before you arrived on my island."

"To talk me out of coming?"

"To see, first, if you were worthy. If you had been an arrogant boor who thought with his fists, I would have taken pleasure in fighting you. But in any case, I had to meet you alone before the battle. As I have said, I will not kill or be killed by a stranger."

"But why wouldn't you tell me who you were?"

She touched his face. "Would you not have suspected trickery if you knew I was to oppose you in combat?"

Remo thought. "Even then, I wouldn't have fought you."

"Because I'm a woman?"

Remo shook his head. "Because . . ." He felt himself trembling.

Stop, he told himself. Don't let yourself fall so hard you'll never pick up the pieces again. But he didn't stop, and he brushed her lips with his own, and felt his loins rush with desire, and then he didn't care if he had to spend the rest of his life regretting this moment, because it was worth whatever price he would have to pay.

His hands filled up with her. He couldn't get close enough. He belonged with her, inside her. Gently he entered her, and her hot flesh welcomed him, smooth, caressing, hungering.

I do love you, he thought. *And I don't care if you can't love me back. This is . . . almost enough. Almost everything I need.* And almost was almost the best thing that had ever happened to him.

"Remo . . ." Jilda breathed, arching him deep into her. "Remo, I love you, too."

With a cry, he let himself flow into her. She held him, strong and sure, their love together burning hot enough to set fire to the stars.

And suddenly Remo knew what he would be willing to give up to keep her with him: everything.

Chapter Seventeen

He slept until the sun was full in the sky and the night mist nearly gone. Jilda kissed him awake.

"Then it wasn't a dream," he said, tangling his fingers in her hair. "What's this?" He lifted the heavy leather cape fastened around her neck. Beneath it was the green dress he'd taken off her the night before. "You're dressed. Is it against your religion to fool around in daylight?"

"Emrys is anxious to get started. We've charted an Arctic course."

He sat up. "How long have I been sleeping?"

"You needed the rest. Everything's been prepared." She handed him a thick sheepskin wrapper. "This is for you. We're heading toward the Irish Sea, then north, over Scandinavia and Russia by water. It will be cold."

Emrys met them half a mile away, a knapsack slung over his shoulders.

"Where's Griffith?" Remo asked. "I wanted to say good-bye to him."

"At home, where he'll stay," Emrys said gruffly. "All weeping and wailing he was. Couldn't stand the sight of him another minute." He walked briskly, his face creased.

"He's a good kid," Remo said.

Emrys grunted.

They reached the shore within the hour. Jilda commandeered the project of building a watertight boat out of wood and twine, covered with animal skins from Emrys's sack.

"We can't go halfway around the world in *that*," Remo complained.

Jilda arched an eyebrow. "When we need another, we will build another," she said.

Never question the logic of a Viking, Remo thought.

It was noon by the time they all settled into the boat. Remo pushed it out of the shallows and jumped in. The small square sail Jilda had brought with her caught the wind and carried them quickly toward the gray, tossing waters of the deep.

Someone shouted, far away, on the shore.

"Who is that?" Jilda said, straining to make out the small figure who ran to the edge of the water, waving his arms frantically overhead.

"By Mryddin, it's the boy," Emrys muttered, standing up shakily. "Go back!" He slapped at the air with his big hands. "Damn you, Griffith, I told you not to follow!"

"Take me with you, Da!" the boy shrieked. "I must be with you. The spirits have told me. Come back, I beg you, Da!"

Shaking a fist at his son, Emrys sat down with a thump that rocked the boat precariously. "Disobedient imp. I'm shamed by the lad, truly shamed."

"He loves you very much," Jilda said. She stood up. "Very much. Look."

Throwing off his shoes, the boy splashed into the water and started swimming the long distance to the boat.

"Is he in the water?" Emrys boomed, trying to rise. "I can't see that far." Jilda pushed him down. The big man's face was strained with worry. "Ah, I suppose he'll give up soon enough and go home," he said with a forced casual air.

The boy swam, a half-mile, a mile. The boat sailed further out to sea, the distance between it and Griffith growing longer with each minute, but the boy continued to flail doggedly on course.

"Is he still coming?" Emrys asked nervously.

"He is."

"Fool. Thinks he'll catch us."

Jilda watched the tiny swimmer, her dress blowing in the gusting wind. "No. He knows he cannot catch us," she said quietly. "All the same, he will not give up." She crossed her arms in front of her. "I was wrong about that one. He calls himself a coward, but his spirit has the strength of ten warriors." She watched him silently for fully another five minutes while Emrys snorted and shifted in his seat, pretending unconcern for his son. Then, without warning, Jilda stripped off the leather cape she wore around her shoulders, and her shoes of sewn skin, and the green dress that fluttered like a sail, until she stood naked on the bow of the boat.

"What in the hell are you doing?" Remo shouted. "Let's just turn the boat around, for God's sake—"

"The boy will not live long enough for that. I have seen drowning men before." She jumped high into the air and dived. She hit the water like a knife, without a ripple, emerging a hundred yards away. With smooth, long strokes she swam to him and carried him back in her arms to the boat.

"Da," Griffith gasped breathlessly as he climbed in. "The Lady of the Lake! The Lady of the Lake came for me. The spirits said I would be protected."

"Silence," Emrys roared, swatting the boy with the back of his hand. "We've lost a whole day because of your foolish ways. Now we'll have to take you back."

"He comes with us," Jilda said.

"Ah, no. I'll not be hampered by such a one as talks to ghosts and tries to drown himself." He coughed politely, handing Jilda her dress. "I'll thank you, though, for saving his life, miss. Not that he deserved it."

Jilda took the dress, but made no attempt to put it on. "He is one of great faith. Perhaps we will need that in the days to come. My people, too, believe in spirits." She slipped on her shoes. "I will look after him," she said.

She dressed quickly, utterly unself-conscious of her nakedness. Her hair, wet and sparkling in the sunshine, looked as if it belonged to a sea nymph. Her eyes had changed color again to match the steel blue of the water.

"Sam, Jilda, Gullikona," Remo recited. "Are you the Lady of the Lake, too?"

The steel eyes smiled slyly. "I am what I must be," she said. "Like all of us."

Out of the corner of his eye, Remo saw Emrys fumbling to put his arm around the shivering, beaming boy.

Chapter Eighteen

A negotiation was underway on the campus of Du Lac College in Minnesota. The two-story ivory-colored mansion that was the home of the college president was ringed by a squad of thirty National Guardsmen, carrying rifles, and staring at a small hillock thirty yards away where two men were talking.

Behind the two men was a crowd of 300 students, dressed in the 1980s version of sixties Greenwich Village chic. There were a lot of bandanas and ripped T-shirts, along with designer jeans and hair died orange and purple and green.

Smith moved into the crowd of students who parted to make way for him, then closed in to swallow him up.

"Who are you?" a female student asked.

"Dr. Feldmar's assistant," Smith said. "She around?"

"Like I haven't seen Birdie yet. She ought to be here."

"Like this is her show, right?" Smith said.

"Yeah."

Smith looked toward the small grassy knoll halfway toward the college president's mansion.

One of the two men there was Smith's age, but he wore cutoff jeans, and a flowered shirt with a black bandana around his open throat. The other man was younger but conservatively dressed in a sports jacket, dress shirt and slacks.

Smith moved through the crowd so he could hear the two men talking.

"We want an end to racism on campus," the older man was saying. He looked bored.

Smith said to a young woman standing next to him, "Who is that guy?" The young woman was bouncing a rock the size of a chicken egg up and down on the palm of her hand.

"That's Vishnu," she said.

"Who's Vishnu?"

"Who are you anyway?" the woman asked suspiciously.

"Robin's assistant," Smith said. "I'm new here."

"Oh. I guess it's all right then. Vishnu's the chairman of the ERA movement. Vishnu's not really his name, but it was his name last year when he was God, and everybody liked the name, and he kept it even if he isn't God anymore."

"ERA?" Smith said. "Equal rights?"

"Naaah," she said in disgust. "End Racist America. It's our new movement. Turn America over to Cuba as a colony."

"Good idea," Smith said.

"Robin's idea," the woman said.

"Who's the other man?" Smith asked.

"Jeez, you don't know anything. That's President McHale."

"He's younger than Vishnu," Smith said.

"We're against ageism," she said. "Students don't have to be young."

The two men on the small knoll were arguing now. The college president said, "What racism?"

"We want black professors in every department."

"We've got them," President McHale said.

"Tokens," Vishnu said. "Meaningless tokens. What about Agent Orange?"

"What about it?"

"What have you done about it?" Vishnu demanded.

"We've kept it off campus," McHale said.

"Words. More words. What about dioxin?"

"What the hell have we got to do with dioxin?" McHale demanded.

"What did you ever do about it?"

"What did *you* ever do about it?"

"I'm not on trial here," Vishnu said.

"I didn't know I was either," McHale said.

"What about AIDS?"

"Campus health center's got a program."

"More words. Just words," Vishnu said. "All that's necessary for evil to triumph is for people like you to do nothing."

"What do you want me to do?" McHale asked.

"It is not for us to dictate your responses."

"Since when? You try to dictate everything else."

Smith had heard enough. He turned back to the young woman. "Where is Robin?" he asked.

"She wanted to be with us today, but she had other business."

Smith was reminded of reluctant generals in World War II who were always bemoaning the fact that they wouldn't be able to go over the top with their men when the shooting started.

"What business?" Smith asked. "I thought everything she did was here."

"Robin's a leader," the young woman said. "She's got

organizations all over the country. Not just this one. We're small.''

The student leader turned his back on President McHale and pulled a paper from his pocket. He looked at the students massed a few yards away from him, then turned back to the college president.

''Our leader,'' Vishnu said, ''warned us of this. She said and she told me to repeat it to you: that this fascistic, imperialistic, genocidal college administration . . .''

McHale snapped, ''What genocidal, for Christ's sake? This is Minnesota. What genocide?''

''You'll find out when the war crimes tribunal convenes.''

''What war crimes? What war?''

''Crimes against Mother Earth; crimes against humanity in the never-ending war between evilness and rightness.''

''Oh, go fuck a grass-filled duck,'' the college president said and stomped away, back toward the national guardsmen still standing impassively along the front of his mansion.

Vishnu turned toward the rest of the students. From this vantage point, Smith could see that Vishnu dyed his thinning hair to cover the gray.

''Our leader warned that this genocidal, fascistic college would not listen to our just pleas,'' Vishnu said. ''And she gave me this to read to you.'' He cleared his throat and began to read.

'' 'I had so wanted to be with you today when the forces of all that is good on earth confront the forces of all that is evil and sick in evil and sick America. I cannot be here, but you must carry on as if I was.

'' 'There comes a time in the lives of all when they must stand for freedom. Cowards might cry peace at any price but the brave and those who would be truly free in this evil nation know that there are times when one must fight to secure persondom's rights. In the interests of

ERA, in the battle against dioxin and Agent Orange and other terrible poisons being injected into our bodies without our consent, in the fight against genocide against our yellow brothers, black brothers, and our Third World brothers, who hold the moral hopes of all mankind, we must never surrender. We must stand and fight. We must let our wisdom and our love shine through.' ''

Vishnu looked up and put the paper back inside his shirt.

"Will we be poisoned?" he yelled.

"No," the students roared.

"Will we kill as they want us to be killers?"

"No," came another roar.

"Will we surrender to this fascist regime, a representative on our beloved campus of an even more fascist regime in Washington?"

"No, no, no," came back the roars.

"Will we fill the world with our love?" Vishnu yelled.

"Yes."

Vishnu turned and looked at the college president's home, then raised his arm over his head like a wagon master and brought it down, pointing toward the mansion.

"Then let's trash this fucking dump," Vishnu yelled.

Rocks suddenly began to fly toward the guardsmen standing near the mansion. The young woman next to Smith tossed her rock, with an obscene curse, then pulled more from the pockets of her jeans. She handed one to Smith.

"Here. You too. From the goodness of the earth."

"Thank you," Smith said. He held the rock in his hand. No one was paying any attention to him. They were tossing rocks and screaming, the crowd taking on a life of its own, seeming to swell, then recede, swell, then recede, like an engine pumping its way up to top running speed. It was only a few moments, Smith thought, before they had worked themselves up into enough of a frenzy to storm the building. And maybe those inexperienced guardsmen facing them might just fire those guns. The guardsmen were now wincing and dodging as rocks began to strike them.

Vishnu was waving his arm in circles about his head. Smith saw his throat muscles working. The next thing would be a command to charge.

Smith backed off two steps, fired his rock, and walked away through the crowd. Behind him, he heard a groan. He felt the students surge past him, moving forward. Twenty yards away, he turned around.

His stone had hit the mark. Vishnu lay on the grass, unconscious, students kneeling around him, ministering to him. On the steps of his home, President McHale nodded, and an ambulance sped forward to take God to a hospital. Campus police came out of the presidential mansion and in the confusion began breaking the students up into small, manageable groups, and then dispersing them.

And Smith walked away. His tape recorders had said that "B" was in charge of the murder plans. "B" for Birdie? Robin Feldmar's students called her "Birdie."

He went back to the professor's locked office. Dr. Robin Feldmar, director, department of computer science. When he was sure no one was in the hall to watch, he slammed the heel of his shoe against the hollow-core door, and it sprang open as the flimsy wood of the frame gave way.

There was a pistol in the back of Robin Feldmar's center desk drawer. Neatly arranged on a piece of paper were two chewed pieces of gum. Apparently, Robin Feldmar chewed gum and then saved it for later. There was no address book, no appointment book, but there was a small handwritten memo.

"United Airlines, 9 A.M. to New York. Earth Goodness. See Mildred."

Smith left the campus for the airport.

Back to New York. And when he let his thoughts get off Robin Feldmar for a moment, he found himself looking forward to seeing Mildred Pensoitte again.

Chapter Nineteen

The Dutchman opened his eyes, frightened. Above him was smooth rock. The place he was in was fragrant. Cool cloths covered his forehead and neck. A thin, long-fingered hand brought a wooden ladle of water to his lips. He tried to push it away but was too weak. He drank.

Squinting to focus, he made out the wrinkled, frowning old Oriental face above him with its hazel eyes and white hair.

"Chiun," he whispered.

"Can you hear?"

The Dutchman nodded.

"You have been unconscious for several days. You must try to eat." Chiun brought over a bowl of rice mixed with warm tea and held it out to him.

"Why do you offer me food?" the Dutchman asked, straining to raise his head.

Chiun propped a pillow of hops and dried leaves behind his patient. "Because you are hungry."

The young man brought the bowl to his lips, his hands shaking. Chiun steadied them with his own.

"You are a fool. Don't you know who I am?"

"You have not changed so much, Jeremiah. I can guess why you have come." Chiun set down the bowl beside him.

"And you think, I suppose, that I will spare your life for a bowl of rice?"

"No," Chiun said softly.

The Dutchman let his head fall back on the pillow. "So you plan to kill me while I am too weak to use my powers. You have some sense, at least."

"I cannot."

The Dutchman's eyes flashed. "What will you do with me?"

"I will care for you until you are well." He brought over a basin of cold water and changed the towels on the Dutchman's head. There was a long silence.

"Why?" he asked, searching the old man's face.

Chiun shook his head. "I fear you would not understand."

H'si T'ang walked inside the cave, a basket of herbs in his hands.

"Who is that?" the Dutchman asked.

Chiun looked to his old teacher, afraid for him. "No one you need to know," he said.

But the blind man shuffled forward. "I am H'si T'ang," he said.

"H'si T'ang, the healer?"

"So they once called me."

"You are blind."

The old Master nodded. "In one way."

"It is said you can see the future. Why did you not set a trap for me?"

H'si T'ang looked at him sadly. "My son, there is none living who is more trapped than you."

"Go away!" the Dutchman shouted hoarsely, his thin face ravaged. "I have no need of your useless ministrations.

Or the feeble philosophies of a blind old relic. I have come to kill you, and when I am able, I will kill you. I promise that!'' He shivered, his teeth chattering.

H'si T'ang turned his back and walked away. Silently Chiun covered the Dutchman with a thin blanket.

"Leave me, I said!'' His eyes were squeezed shut in a grimace. A tear trickled over the skin of his temple into his hair.

Chiun left his side, and the Dutchman slept.

He awoke after nightfall. His eyes adjusted automatically to the darkness of the cave. He tested his fingers. They worked. The rice had given him enough strength to move. He pushed aside the damp rags on his forehead. There was no fever now.

The blind one was gone. Chiun sat a few feet away in lotus position, his eyes closed. Watching him, the Dutchman carefully removed the blanket that covered him and rose. The Oriental didn't awaken.

He stole toward the sleeping figure with movements so controlled that even the air around him was not disturbed. Then, bending low, he prepared his attack.

Chiun's eyes opened wide. There was not a trace of grogginess or confusion in them. Expectant, alert, knowing, they seemed to take in the Dutchman's very thoughts at a glance.

The Dutchman stopped, his jaw dropping.

"Why do you hesitate?'' Chiun said sharply.

The Dutchman felt his breathing come faster. "I—I—''

"Can you kill only sleeping victims? Have you been reduced to that?''

The Dutchman backed away, trembling. "It would have been easier,'' he said. "Master, I do not wish to kill you.'' It was a cry of desperation. "But I must. It was my vow to Nuihc. While you live, I will never find rest. It was his curse upon me.''

"Nuihc lied to you. You will not find the peace you seek by killing me."

"You are wrong," he said passionately. "He will free me then. I will be permitted to die."

Chiun looked at the miserable, thin man with his hunched shoulders. He remembered that he had once been a beautiful youth with a quick, fine mind and hands as fast as the wind.

"Even then, you wanted to die," Chiun said absently. "Did you never try to end your life?"

The Dutchman laughed, the sound thin and bitter. "I cannot count the times. But it won't let me, this——" He pounded his chest with his fist as if it were a distasteful alien thing.

"The power," Chiun said.

"It is a greater curse than the fires of hell. It will only leave me after your death."

Chiun shook his head sadly. "Nuihc knew that you were born with abilities beyond the scope of others. By not teaching you to control your power, he guessed that it would drive you to fulfill his purpose. He tricked you, Jeremiah. There will be no rest for you. The power is too strong by now."

"Liar!" His arm struck out at Chiun. The attack was swift, with the perfect form Chiun remembered. At the moment before the side of his hand made contact with the old Oriental's face, he screamed and lurched backward, off balance. Aghast, he looked up. Behind Chiun, in a low doorway leading to an adjoining chamber of the cave, stood the blind H'si T'ang. The old man stood stock still, his face expressionless.

"The power," the Dutchman whispered. "You have it, too."

H'si T'ang turned and walked back into the shadows, his hands clasped together.

The Dutchman's eyes remained fixed on the spot where the old man had stood. "But it has not . . ."

"Destroyed him?" Chiun finished. "No. He has not used it as you have."

The young man's eyes widened in pain. "You mean it was not necessary . . . I could have . . ."

"It is too late to think of those things now," Chiun said gently.

The Dutchman swallowed. *All the suffering, for nothing!* It could have been prevented. The power could have been controlled, the beast silenced.

"Nuihc knew?" he asked numbly.

"Yes," Chiun said. "He knew. I am sorry."

The young man staggered backward toward the cave entrance, brushing the back of his hand across his eyes. "You were stupid to let me live," he said brokenly. "I am not strong enough to kill you now, but I will be soon. And then I will come back for you. I'll kill you then, old man, do you understand? I'll kill you."

He rushed out into the night.

H'si T'ang emerged. "You have done a good job of nursing our visitor," he said, smiling. "My poor powers were strained nearly to breaking just to halt his attack on you. I am too old to attempt these exertions. The boy is stronger than he believes."

"He knows how strong he is," Chiun said. "He could have attacked me again after you left. Or he could have used his powers against me. He spared my life because I spared his." He looked toward the cave entrance. "The pity is that he was born to be a decent man. Even Nuihc's evil could not erase all his decency."

"Will he not return?"

"Oh, he will return." Outside, he heard the Dutchman's careless, stumbling footfalls. "You see, he believes that killing me is his only chance to find peace. He cannot accept that he has no chance at all.''

H'si T'ang lit a candle for Chiun's benefit, and the two Masters drank tea. For a long time, past many miles, Chiun could still hear the Dutchman, weeping.

Chapter Twenty

Nuihc, you could have helped me.

The Dutchman stumbled across the sandy, grass-tufted earth, oblivious to the deep snake holes. He just wanted to run, to crawl into the night like a small blind animal.

I thought of you as my father. I spent my life trying to please you.

He had learned the exercises Nuihc had given him. He had practiced until his fingers were bloody and his body ached for months on end. He had been both son and servant to the dark-eyed man who had said he came to save him. And the whole time, he now realized, Nuihc had seen Jeremiah's torment as the boy struggled with the extraordinary mental gift he had been born with, and had ignored it.

Nuihc knew how to control the beast. And he never told me.

He draped himself over a boulder and cried.

But the old man had the power, too.

He raised his head. *He wasn't the only one.* H'si T'ang's old body housed a beast, too, only he could control it.

Maybe the old man's power wasn't as strong as his own, but the fact was, it belonged to him. The beast didn't own H'si T'ang.

Was it possible? The Dutchman sat up slowly, his senses tingling. Could he, too, learn how to use his gift only when he decided? It would take effort, and time . . .

His mind raced. He was sane now. Otherwise, he could never have walked out of the cave without lashing out at Chiun with the power. It was the first time he'd felt sane since before the incident with the girl in the Russian forest. It must have been the long rest, or Chiun's care, or the atmosphere of the cave itself. Whatever it was, though, it would pass quickly. He knew his beast. It would not leave him alone for long.

Think. Think quickly, while you have time.

Maybe Chiun was right. Nuihc had deceived him about his power. Maybe his promise that the Dutchman would find rest after killing Chiun was just another lie. In the past, killing had only led the Dutchman to more killing. The destructive power fed on itself. With each murder, the need for others grew in him. Why should it be any different with Chiun, who had saved his life and above all others that deserved to live?

If he could just go away somewhere, think, study. He had lived a lifetime of spartan discipline. Surely, with time, he could confront the beast and tame it. Surely . . .

He heard the commands of a North Korean patrol as they tramped over a hill. Maneuvers, he guessed. There were only six of them, carrying weapons and dressed in combat fatigues. He crouched on the ground, waiting for them to pass, but they spotted him.

"You there!" the leader called.

No. Not now, the Dutchman thought. *I must be left alone now.* The time was too short. He had to escape with the beast still in its flimsy cage.

"Your papers, please," the leader of the patrol snapped, approaching him.

"I don't—"

"No papers? What is your purpose here?"

The Dutchman stepped backward slowly. He closed his eyes. The colors . . . "Leave me," he said, choking.

The leader laughed harshly. "Arrogant white dung. What makes you think you can walk around with no identification? Filthy spy." He shoved the Dutchman. "You're coming with us."

He shook. The colors were brighter. Wild, frightening music sang in his ears. His vision clouded, then sprang into sharp, brilliant focus.

"Look at him trembling. This is how decadent western spies fall to pieces when confronted with the people's might." He thrust his rifle butt between the Dutchman's shoulderblades.

Get away. Now. Before it's too late.

He ran. Behind him, the leader shouted orders to his men. They fired. The Dutchman set up a pattern of anti-rhythm, moving so erratically that the bullets could not reach him. He ran, with the patrol following behind shouting, their weapons echoing through the hills. When he was far enough ahead of them, he changed the pattern. Anti-rhythm was difficult. It strained his sense of balance. He loped along, following the scent of the sea. Even if he had to swim, he would leave this place immediately. There was hope, somewhere, if he could just get away.

He tripped over a deep hole and went sprawling on the grass. The fall knocked the wind out of him, but his head didn't strike ground. His hands gripped the edge of a dirt precipice. Below him, just beneath his head, slithered a swarm of snakes.

The sight startled him, but he made no move to leave the edge of the pit. There must have been more than a hundred of the creatures, some as wide as his arm. Seeing him, the snakes coiled and darted in a frenzy, their mouths opening to accommodate their long, hinged vipers' teeth.

He remained, fascinated, watching, as the Korean soldiers approached from behind.

Creatures of my own kind. Like me, you inflict death as a matter of course. Like mine, your power is beyond your own understanding. But I know you, because I am like you, despised, unwelcome among the gentler beings of the earth. You and I, my friends, we are the children of fear.

He gave up. There was no point in escaping now. Quietly, deep inside him, the beast's cage clicked open and flooded him with relief.

The soldiers were close behind him now, crouching, their weapons raised. The Dutchman almost laughed out loud at their clumsy efforts to move silently. He could hear their quickened breathing, the sound of their fingers on the metal and wood of their rifles.

Leaping upward in a spiral, he knocked the weapon out of the leader's hands and kicked him in the throat. Bright blood spurted out of the Korean's mouth. He fell in a heap, his arms and legs akimbo. Rushing the other startled soldiers, the Dutchman struck a finger into a man's eye, gouging deep into the brain tissue. He caught the third by both legs and, shouting to the music ringing in his ears, tore him in two.

The others tried to run. "Oh, no," he said, smiling. He swept his arm past his field of vision. The soldiers, now aglow in pulsating light, stopped in their tracks.

"Come here," he said. The men obeyed.

He nodded, and the music focused into a pinpoint of shattering sound. The men covered their ears, shrieking. Blood oozed from between their fingers.

"Go to the snakes."

The men cried out, but their legs kept moving. One fell

on his knees, crawling behind the others. One by one, they drew themselves to the edge of the pit and stumbled in.

The snakes were ready.

They attacked in a mass, jerking and writhing convulsively, their yellow fangs sinking deep into the flesh of the screaming men. The Dutchman stood at the edge of the pit, his arms crossed in front of his chest. A thin stream of saliva fell from the corners of his mouth. When the last faint cries of pain had died away, he lay down slowly beside the gaping hole in the ground. The snakes seemed to throb with the rhythm of their own destructiveness.

"My brothers," he whispered, extending his hand over the pit. The vipers slowed and grew still. He raised his arm. Slowly, its eyes opening and closing sluggishly, the largest of the snakes left the ground and floated upward, weightless, out of the pit. He coiled the snake around his own body, where the creature crawled in a lethargic dance over his neck and face, around his upraised arms, between his legs.

The Dutchman was sweating. The pleasure of the snake's movements was exquisite, better than any woman. Its dry scales carried the scent of death on them. With his tongue, the Dutchman licked the animal's belly. Moaning, he descended into the pit, the viper wound around his waist. He lay there for some time, surrounded by the staring eyes and open mouths of the dead men, while the snakes curled around him like smoke.

Chapter Twenty-One

Mildred Pensoitte smiled when Smith walked into her office in midafternoon.

"How is my resident genius now that he's back in residence?" she asked.

"I'm fine. I just had a very unusual call."

"Oh?" she said.

"Some man called for a Robin Feldmar. He said he wanted to give Earth Goodness a large donation, but he'd only give it to Robin Feldmar and only personally."

"Oh. That's odd." Her brow furrowed. "Did he say anything else?"

"He said that Robin Feldmar would know how to use the money right to get rid of imperialists." Smith said. "He said he knew her well."

"Did he give a name?" she asked.

"No. He said he'd call back." Smith shrugged. "Do you know a Robin Feldmar? I can't find a record on her anywhere."

Dr. Pensoitte was looking out the window as if Smith were not even in her office. Then she turned back to him with a slow, growing smile.

"Sure, Harry. Of course I do. She was one of my college professors. The first one who got me involved with the environment."

"And she's with Earth Goodness, Inc.?" Smith asked.

"She helped me found it in the early days," Mildred said.

"Okay," Smith said. "Is she around?" He tried a smile and realized how rarely it was that he smiled because his face felt sore as he attempted it. "We can't afford to go turning down large contributions."

"As luck would have it, she's in town," Mildred said. "We're having dinner tonight."

"Good."

"So when that man calls back, get his name and number and tell him that we'll have Birdie call him."

Smith nodded.

"What did he sound like?" Mildred asked.

"What do you mean?" asked Smith in return.

"You think he might have been a crank? Birdie gets bothered a lot by cranks."

"He sounded very substantial," Smith said.

"Good, Harry. I like substantial," she said. "As I said, Birdie gets bothered a lot. She even gets death threats."

"From whom?" Smith asked.

Mildred shrugged. "Cranks, I guess. Because she's so active in so many organizations to make America live up to its promise."

Smith thought of the young students he had seen that day in Minnesota, set up by Robin Feldmar to use as cannon fodder, and he wished he could tell Dr. Pensoitte that her friend was a faker and a fraud. But he could not do that. Not yet. Not unless he wanted to admit also that the so-called telephone message and the anonymous giver were also just lies—just to find out where Robin Feldmar could be located.

"Substantial," she said.

"What?" Smith asked.

"We were just talking about substantial. You know, Harry, that's what you are."

"It's what I try to be," he said. He smiled again and found it easier this time. Maybe it just took practice.

"That's why I need you," she said. "Earth Goodness needs you. You have a future here with us."

"You think so?"

"I know so. We're just starting. We're going to be one of the biggest groups in international affairs in just a few more years, and we need management to do that. We need you, Harry. Earth Goodness needs you. I need you. The world needs you."

"That's very flattering," he said.

"And very true. You said you were bored. I can promise that you'll never be bored around here," she said.

"I can already see that."

She smiled at him. Her eyes were very dark. "I'll never let you be bored."

"I hope not."

"I suspect you'll be working late tonight? As usual?" she asked and Smith nodded.

"Well, I'm going to go home. When you finish up, why don't you come over? You can meet Robin Feldmar. And if you've got that unknown benefactor's name and number, Birdie can call him right away."

Before she left, she gave Smith the address of her apartment building on Manhattan's Upper West Side.

Smith sat alone in his darkened office, a circle of light from a gooseneck lamp on his desk the only illumination for a hundred feet in each direction. Everyone else had gone. It had been his experience that the more anarchist and anti-establishment an organization's goals were, the more likely its office staff would be clock-punchers. At 4:30 P.M., the workers had fled like a toilet being flushed.

He was on the telephone with the computers at Folcroft. Nobody had been killed or seriously injured at Du Lac college that day, and news reports said that fast action by the college president had succeeded in averting a major tragedy.

Smith shook his head. The real major tragedy was that so many young people in college were having their heads filled with slogans, instead of learning to think for themselves.

The computer had received no messages from the assassins' network about the four men who had died in St. Martin's. Smith thought for a moment about the men he had killed. The killing had shaken him, and he wished again that Remo and Chiun were available. Did Remo suffer like that when there was a life to be taken? Or did he just go ahead and do his job anyway?

Smith put those thoughts out of his mind and concentrated on what he had learned from the men.

One of them would have been able to monitor Secret Service security messages. That would explain why the Secret Service had not moved to protect the president when Smith had put word of the assassination attempt into their computers.

But that still didn't mean it was safe for the president to return home. Not yet, because even if they were totally on the job, the Secret Service might not be able to protect him from a dedicated assassination team. His return would still have to wait for Smith's dismantling of the assassination crew.

The dead young men's orders had come from Robin Feldmar. And Robin Feldmar had been close with Mildred Pensoitte. And Feldmar managed a computer network at Du Lac College. And she had a history of involvement with radical groups. And her nickname was Birdie, and the assassin leader's initial was "B."

The more he thought of it, the more sure he was that Robin Feldmar had taken over Earth Goodness, without Mildred Pensoitte's knowledge, and used it as a base for her plot to kill the president.

He was cleaning off his desk when the telephone rang.

Mildred Pensoitte's voice crackled with fear. "Oh, Harry, I'm so glad I caught you."

"What's the matter?"

"Please come over here. There's been a terrible tragedy."

"What happened? Are you all right?"

"I'm all right. But Birdie . . . poor Birdie is dead."

Smith met Mildred in the lobby of one of New York City's largest hotels, which offered getaway weekends at special rates for people and roaches. She took his arm and led him to the elevators, but the elevator car was crowded, and she said nothing until she unlocked the door to a room on the eighth floor and stepped aside so he could enter.

Robin Feldmar had been a tall, attractive woman in her late forties. But now, with her throat cut from one ear to another in a grim, ghastly echo of a smile, she was just a tall, bloodied corpse, lying on the floor of her room near the foot of a bed.

"What happened?" Smith asked.

"I got here to pick her up and bring her to my place for dinner," Mildred said. "She didn't answer the phone, so I thought she was in the shower, and I came up. The door was open a crack, and when I pushed it open, I saw her body. She was dead. Oh, Harry." She collapsed against Smith, who held her against his chest, patting the back of her head gently, uncomfortably aware of her bosom heaving against his chest. It was an unusual feeling, holding and comforting a woman. He could not ever remember having held Irma that way.

Smith looked past Mildred at the room. All the drawers were still closed, and clothing hung neatly in an open closet. There was no indication that the room had been ransacked.

"Did you call me from here?" he asked.

"No. I ran first," she said. "Then I thought better and called you from the lobby."

"Did you touch anything?" he said.

She looked confused, and tears coursed down her face. She shook her head. "Just the door, I guess. And the key."

"Be sure," he said. "Did you use the bathroom? Did you go in there to throw up?"

"No. No." She started to turn away from Smith, saw the body on the floor again, and turned back to him sobbing. She threw her arms over his shoulders and around his neck.

"I'm sorry. I guess I'm just no good at this."

"Here's what I want you to do," Smith said. "Dry your eyes, go downstairs, walk a few blocks away, and then take a cab home. I'll meet you there in a little while."

"What are you going to do?"

"I want to make sure that you haven't dropped anything here or left anything. Then I'll follow you."

"We're not going to call the police?" she said.

"Feldmar's dead," Smith said. "Why should you be involved? It'd only hurt the organization."

She looked at him silently, then nodded. "I guess you're right."

"I know I'm right. Go ahead. I'll meet you at your apartment."

She ran quickly from the room, and the door swung shut behind her. Smith stood with his back to the entrance door and visualized what a woman might do if she came into a room and saw her friend dead on the floor, a murder victim.

He quickly stepped forward to the body and knelt along-side it. Almost without thought, his hand reached out to the wooden base of the bed to steady himself. With his handkerchief, he carefully wiped the wooden base clean of fingerprints.

Kneeling there, he looked at the body. There was a puncture wound under the left ear and then a slow jagged rip across the throat to under the right ear. He had seen that kind of wound before. It was administered by some-one who came from behind the victim, threw an arm around her, and then with his right hand drove the knife into her throat and slashed from left to right. The wound was jagged, the flesh almost serrated. It had been a dull knife, and the killer had had to saw his way around Robin Feldmar's throat. It had taken a long time, and it demon-strated a lot of hate or anger, he thought.

The room key was back on the dresser where Mildred had put it, and he wiped the plastic tag free of prints. He walked back to the door, wiping his handkerchief along the edge of the dresser where Mildred might have rested a hand if she had stumbled or paused for a moment in her panic. He cleaned the doorknob, then with his handker-chief opened the door and listened for sound in the hallway. There was none, so he stepped into the hallway. The heavy door swung shut behind him and clicked. He wiped the doorknob, put his handkerchief back in his pocket, and walked quickly away down the hall.

He went out a side door of the hotel and walked for two blocks before hailing a cab to Mildred Pensoitte's apartment.

While he was riding the thirty blocks uptown, he won-dered who would have wanted to kill Robin Feldmar. It would have been an easy problem if he had been one of her disciples: he could have believed that she was killed by the big, repressive, all-powerful government who wanted to silence her voice. But more than anyone else in America, Smith knew that was wrong, because he was the person inside the government who authorized the killing of people because they represented a danger to that government.

The killer was someone else.

But who?

"But who would have wanted to kill her?" he asked Mildred at her apartment. She had regained her composure somewhat and had changed into a long flowing robe. They sat across a pot of coffee in her living room. Smith had declined her offer of something to eat.

"I guess I'd better tell you everything," Mildred said.

"I think so."

Mildred walked to a sideboard, poured herself a small glass of cream sherry, and when she came back, sat on the sofa alongside Smith. She sipped her drink and put it on the table in front of them.

"Birdie was more than just my friend," Mildred said. "When I was a graduate student, I worked with her at the college. I started the Earth Goodness Society, but it was her idea."

"I see," Smith said.

"And she stayed active in it. Most of our long-range planning, well, she did on her computers back at the school. She had worked out a program. . . . Well, it's much too complicated for me; I could never really understand what she was talking about. But somehow it measured the potential of various public situations and told us where we ought to concentrate our efforts to get maximum public exposure and do maximum public good."

She stopped to sip her drink, then stared away across the room.

"If the organization was her idea, why didn't she run it?" Smith finally asked.

"Birdie wasn't like that. She liked to plan and brainstorm and think, but she had no follow-through. She didn't want anything to do with administration. She was always starting different groups, leading different causes. She had a brilliant mind but no staying power." She hesitated, then added, "Sometimes, though, I thought she always kept a hand in Earth Goodness, because she often seemed to know more about what it was doing than I did."

"When did she tell you she was coming to New York?"

"I was coming to that," Mildred said. She extended her legs up onto the coffee table. Her long, shiny robe clung to the outline of her calves, and Smith forced himself to look away. "She called me yesterday," Mildred said. "This is the frightening part. She said that she had uncovered information that someone had infiltrated our organization, somebody dangerous."

"Exactly what did she say?" Smith asked.

"She said that four of our followers had just been killed in St. Martin's for no reason at all. She was afraid that they were killed by someone who had gotten their names from inside Earth Goodness."

"Did she have any idea of who infiltrated our society?" Unconsciously, Smith clenched his hands between his legs.

"No," Mildred said and his hands relaxed.

"What did you think of all this?" he asked.

Mildred turned to look at him. Her eyes were warm, and she had a small, sad smile at the corners of her mouth.

"Birdie was given sometimes to exaggeration. Honestly, I didn't think anything of it. I thought it was another one of her the-sky-is-falling stories. And now . . . now, she's dead."

She pressed her face forward against Smith, and he reached out to put his arm around her shoulder.

"There, there," he said. "Would you have any idea why anybody would want to infiltrate Earth Goodness?"

"No. Why would anyone?"

"There aren't any secret projects going on that might have upset some corporation bigwigs somewhere?" Smith said. "Nothing that might have created enemies for us?"

"No," she said. "We do everything in public. There wasn't anything." She hesitated. "Not unless Birdie was doing something I didn't know anything about."

He felt her sobbing gently against him.

"Easy," he said. "It'll be all right."

"She's dead. My friend's dead. I'm afraid, Harry. If someone's in our organization who's a killer, I'm afraid. Maybe I'm next."

"I won't let anything happen to you," Smith said. She felt good and warm next to him, and he squeezed her shoulder slightly.

"Stay with me," she said.

"I will."

"I mean tonight. Stay here with me."

"I don't . . ."

"I don't want to be alone," she said. "Stay with me." He felt her hands reach up to his face and touch his cheeks. She turned his head toward her and then reached up and kissed him on the mouth. For a moment, he considered his position. He was a married man. A father. A man on a mission. He had no time for such things; no right to engage in them. And another voice inside his head said, *You are also a man*, and he surrendered himself to Mildred Pensoitte's kiss.

"That was nice," she said when she pulled away from him.

"Yes," he said. It was nice and he was a man, but he was still a husband, a father, and a man with a mission.

There would be no more of that tonight, he told himself sternly.

"Do you think it was all right that we ran away from Birdie's room?" she asked.

"I think you had to do it. Otherwise you'd be dragged into the mud by the press. The society might be hurt too," he said.

"You understand things like that, Harry," she said. "Almost as if you had done them before."

"An active imagination," Smith said.

Mildred smiled at him, then rose and walked from the room, leaving Smith to sit in silence, thinking.

He was supposed to be finding a presidential assassin, and here he was playing kissy-face with a woman. And he had no excuse for it. And what of Irma? Good, sweet, kindly Irma who was back home in Rye, New York, patiently waiting for his return.

Was it fair to her?

He wished that he could reach Remo and Chiun. He had spent so long in his office that now it was a symbol of how he dealt with the world. Shut away from it, and that was best because he did not know how to deal with it. Even the one-way glass in his office windows was a symbol. It let him look out into the world, but reminded him that he should not try to be *of* the world.

He was sure that Remo and Chiun were enjoying themselves somewhere and when they got back, he would certainly have something to say to them about duty and responsibility. And about who was paying the bills.

He glanced at his wristwatch. Night had long ago dropped onto the city, and Mildred had left the room almost forty minutes ago. For a moment, he felt the pang of fear in his throat, and he walked quickly along the hallway outside the living room. He stopped outside a closed door at the end of the hall and called her name.

"Come in," answered her soft voice.

He opened the door. She was in her bed. The room was lit only by a small reading lamp. The sheet of her bed was pulled up to her long, lovely throat.

Her flesh was white and cool-looking.

"I thought you . . . well, I'm sorry. I was wondering if you were all right," he said.

"I thought you'd never come," she said. "Come in."

"No," Smith said. "I just wanted to be sure that everything was okay."

"Everything is not okay."

"No? What's the matter?" he asked.

"It won't be okay until you're here with me, Harry."

He took a step inside the room. Slowly she pulled the sheet down, off her naked body, and extended her arms to him.

He took another step. Then stopped.

"I can't," he said. "I just can't."

"You said you'd stay," she said in a pouting voice. She made no effort to pull the sheet back up.

"I will. I'll stay outside on the sofa. You'll be safe," he promised.

"But will you?" she asked.

Chapter Twenty-Two

It was mid-morning when the travelers from Wales landed in Sinanju.

"Watch for snakes," Remo said.

The boy, Griffith, holding fast to Jilda's hand, looked around at the bleak forbidding, landscape. "So this is the land of the great Chinee," he said, awestruck. "Would they be invisible, now?"

"No, boy," Emrys said. "But watch where you're walking. Hoa, what's wrong?"

The boy sank to his knees, wrapping his thin arms over his head. " 'Tis a—terrible strong force," the boy groaned.

Remo felt dizzy. "I feel it, too. Music." The air was filled with dissonant sounds that were somehow strangely familiar. "There's music coming from somewhere close."

Jilda and Emrys looked at one another. There was no music that they could hear. "Come," she said, picking up the boy in her arms. "You're both tired."

"Can't you hear it?" Remo slapped his hands over his ears. "The loudest music I ever heard. Oh . . ."

He fell. Emrys rushed over to him. "What is it?"

"Can't move." He tried to sit up. Not a muscle worked. Even his fingers were immobile. And the discordant music kept roaring in his ears.

Emrys slid his burly arms beneath Remo and lifted him. "We're near the cave," he said, making his way inland at a trot.

Inside the cave, the music vanished. Griffith got to his feet as H'si T'ang laid hands on Remo. Within a few minutes, Remo sat up.

"The Chinee can make magic," the boy whispered to his father.

"Indeed," Chiun said. "But we are not Chinese. I am Chiun, Master of Sinanju, and this is H'si T'ang, past Master." He gave the boy a small bow.

Griffith returned it as best he could. "I am Griffith, sir. I meant no disrespect."

"Then call us by our proper names."

"Yes, sir," Griffith said meekly.

Remo flexed his hands. "I can't understand it," he said. "I was fine one minute, and then—"

"There are things which must be explained," Chiun said. "But first, why are you here—all of you?" He looked sternly at the four visitors.

"Well, it's uh—" Remo fumbled.

"We have decided not to carry out the Master's Trial," Jilda said.

Chiun's eyebrows rose.

Remo stood up. "That's right. I'm sorry, Little Father, but it's not for me. I beat Ancion and Kiree by luck. I wasn't a better fighter than they were, and I felt rotten afterward. They shouldn't have had to die. I think there's room for all of us on this planet. Jilda and Emrys feel the same way."

Chiun began to sputter, but H'si T'ang intervened. "As do I, my son. I congratulate you all on your intelligence."

"But the Trial," Chiun said, incredulous at the effrontery of the three contestants. "It is one of the oldest traditions in Sinanju."

"The preservation of our people is the oldest tradition," H'si T'ang said, "and the most worthwhile. Do you not see, Chiun? Trial. You needed Remo, and he has come."

"Needed me? What for?"

Chiun settled himself in a sitting position beside Remo. "Do you remember the Dutchman?"

"Sure. He was killed off the coast of St. Martin's."

"No. He lives. He is here." He described his confrontation with the thin man who had arrived unconscious at the cave, and of the Dutchman's exit the night before. "I could not kill him," Chiun said, his eyes lowered. "He is my punishment for the death of Nuihc. That task must rest with you."

"Can he really make things explode just by looking at them?" Griffith asked. Emrys prodded the boy with his elbow.

"Unfortunately, yes," H'si T'ang said. "A very dangerous man."

Remo stood slowly, thinking. "It was him, then. The music, everything. He knows I'm here."

"I'm afraid so," Chiun said.

Remo sighed. "I'd better not waste any time."

Jilda rose. "No," Remo said, cutting her off before she could speak.

"But I didn't hear any music. He won't be after me."

"He will be if you show up."

"Oh—"

"Don't you see? You'd hear the music if he wanted you to hear it. You'd do anything he told you. You just can't fight him, Jilda."

"Can you?"

He looked outside, at the rocky hills beyond the cave. "I don't know," he said, and left.

"I must go with him," Jilda said, rushing after Remo. Chiun stopped her. "The Dutchman is not your adversary. You would surely die in combat with him."

"I'd have as much of a chance as Remo has!"

"No, my child. You are a fine warrior. I have heard of your bravery and skill. But only Remo stands a chance against this man."

"Why Remo?" Emrys asked defensively.

"Because Remo is not who he believes himself to be."

"Who is he, then?" Emrys barely concealed his disdain.

"He is a being beyond the scope of our understanding," Chiun said. "But in order to fulfill his destiny, he must first come to realize this. I had hoped that the Master's Trial would help him to arrive at this knowledge, but it has not. Perhaps he will learn now."

"A lot of mumbo-jumbo, if you ask me," Emrys muttered. "If this Dutchman fella's as much of a maniac as you say, Remo can use my help." He lumbered out of the cave.

"Emrys, don't go!" Jilda shouted. Emrys didn't turn back. She rushed to collect her things. "I'll go, too. If there are three of us . . ." Her gaze rested on Griffith.

The boy was sitting cross-legged, staring into space. "Don't leave, Da," he said quietly. "The power I feel is death, and the music is the song of the beast."

Jilda bent low over him. "Griffith? What are you saying?"

Griffith continued to stare, unblinking.

"The boy understands," said H'si T'ang.

Chapter Twenty-Three

"A being beyond scope," Emrys grumbled. "Doesn't know who he is. My arse."

Remo wasn't any weirder a being than anyone else, except maybe his teachers. Masters of Sinanju or not, those Chinee were a couple of lunatics. No wonder poor Remo couldn't even eat a rabbit. Brought up by crazy men, that's what he was. And with all their magic, not a one between them to help the poor sod out in a fight.

Well, Remo had done his share on the long journey from Wales, and even if he didn't come from the valley, he was as good a friend as Emrys had. He'd find that when he needed help, Emrys would be there to lend a hand.

There he was, just ahead, a form turning the crest of the hill. "Ho, Remo," Emrys called, but his voice was drowned in a wave of swelling music.

Music?

You'd hear the music if he wanted you to hear it, Remo had said.

The music grew louder. Emrys unsheathed his knife and whirled around. Nothing.

But the music . . . Suddenly his feet shifted beneath him. He lunged, but he remained rooted where he stood. His feet were covered to the ankles in soft, bubbling mud the consistency of gruel.

"Quicksand," he whispered, unbelieving. As far as he could see, the dry, grassy soil had turned into a roiling cauldron of yellow muck. He struggled, dropping his knife. It disappeared into the liquid earth.

The figure appeared again on the hill. "Remo!" Emrys called. "By Mryddin, come get me out of this mess!"

The quicksand disappeared. In the blink of an eye, Emrys was standing once again on firm ground. His knife lay beside him in a tuft of grass.

"All the gods," he said. The figure was still standing on the hill, which, inexplicably, seemed to turn blue.

He shook his head. It was a damn good thing he hadn't fought Remo in the Master's Trial, he thought. His vision wasn't just weak, it was playing tricks on him as well.

He walked toward it. The blue of the mound changed to green, and then to violet. The hill itself appeared to change shape, into an impossibly correct geometric pyramid. The low rises around it spiked upward into perfect triangles, glowing in a spectrum of unearthly colors like some modernist stage set.

"This can't be happening," Emrys said. It must have been the sea voyage. He'd heard about sailors who'd claimed to see strange things from being too long off land. And the food had been scant and bad, and . . .

"Your eyes are failing," a voice said, seemingly from nowhere. He turned around, jabbing the air instinctively with his knife.

"Can't you see me?" The voice was smooth, mocking.

"Come out here and fight me like a man."

"But I am here." Emrys whirled back to face the

mountain. Where a moment before had been only empty air now stood a tall blond man with cornflower-blue eyes.

"How—how—"

"It depends on what you see," the man said. "In your case, that isn't much. Why, you're nothing but a stumbling, blind thing. A wounded animal. It would be far too easy to kill you."

"Well, now, why don't you just try it then, you mother-less snake?"

The Dutchman's eyes widened. "You would do better to be afraid."

"The day I'm afraid of a skinny big-mouth fool like you is the day I'm buried in my grave," Emrys said.

"As you wish."

The Dutchman was gone. Then, instantaneously, his lone figure stood once again on the surrealistic mountain. Two birds swept near him, squawking. The Dutchman snatched out with his hands and plucked them out of the sky. Emrys stood poised for battle, beads of sweat forming on his brow.

The Dutchman released the birds. They flew like bullets in a straight line toward Emrys. Halfway to their target, the birds changed into hurtling balls of white light. Emrys swatted at them with his knife, but their speed was faster than anything he'd even seen. The glowing spheres shot into his eyes, burning them to blackened holes. The Welshman screamed once, then fell, his hands covering his head while his body convulsed in pain.

"Da!" Griffith shouted in the cave. He stood up, his hands slapping against his eyes. "My da! He's hurt."

Jilda put her arms around him.

"Let me go!" My da needs me now!" He strained toward the open mouth of the cave.

Jilda breathed deeply. "I'm going," she said.

Chiun nodded, rising.

"We shall all go," H'si T'ang said.

They found Emrys still writhing in pain, the ground where he had fallen kicked up from the movement of his legs.

"Da!" Griffith called, running to him.

H'si T'ang pried open the big man's hands to touch the ugly black wounds where his eyes had been.

Remo came over the hill. "I heard someone," he said. Then he saw Emrys. "Oh, God." The boy had his small arms wrapped around his father.

"Can't you do something?" Remo asked H'si T'ang.

"It is too late," the old man said. "He is dying. There is nothing to be done."

"Jilda . . . Jilda," Emrys whispered, barely able to move his lips.

Jilda knelt beside him. "I am here, my friend."

The Welshman struggled to speak. "Take care of my son," he said. Sweat poured off him. "Take him back home. See that he's safe, I beg you." He clutched her hand.

"I promise," Jilda said. "May the fields be sweet where you walk."

"Griffith . . ."

"Yes, Da, yes," the boy sobbed.

"None of your weeping. You are to take my place, so your job is to stay well and strong."

The boy shook. "Oh, Da, I did it. Your sight's gone because of me. That day in the tree, when you fell—"

"No!" The big man's voice rose. "My blindness was not your doing."

"You fell when you tried to save me," the boy said miserably.

"It wasn't that way, son. I fell, but it was not the rock I hit that ruined my sight. My eyes were going bad long before that, but I said nothing about it. I could not admit my own weakness, don't you know. I let you take the blame, to save my pride."

"No, Da—"

"Yes." His hand groped out to grip the boy's arm. "And you carried the burden like a man. A better man than I ever was. Griffith . . ." He was heaving now with the effort of breathing.

The boy pressed his head against his father's and whispered in his ear. "I can hear you, Da."

"Trust your spirits. They've made you fine. Ask them to forgive me, if you can." He kissed his son.

As gently as he could, Remo lifted up the giant and walked with him in his arms. For a moment, Emrys managed a thin smile. "You're not half bad for a Chinee," he said. His head fell back. The cave was in sight.

"He's dead," Remo said quietly.

Chapter Twenty-Four

Mildred Pensoitte was asleep. Smith had peeked into her room to be sure of it, then had closed the door tightly, and now he sat at a small desk in the far corner of the living room. He kept his back toward the front windows. If Mildred should awaken and come into the room, he could see her and hang up the telephone before she noticed anything.

He unlocked his attaché case with the small brass key he kept pinned to the fabric of an inside jacket pocket. From the case, he took a small round device that looked, in shape, like a two-inch-thick slab cut from a piece of liverwurst. It was an invention of his own design. On the top of the device were keys, marked with letters and numbers, and when he telephoned into the computers at Folcroft, he could spell out questions, and they would answer back, by electronic signals, depressing the printing keys, and the answer would be recorded on micro-thin paper stored inside the unit.

The phone was a pushbutton telephone with several lines. It didn't matter. Even if Mildred should pick up an extension in her bedroom, all she would hear would be electronic tones.

Smith dialed the local access code for the Folcroft computers. He had recently improved the design of his telephone system so now it was possible to reach his computers through a local call from anywhere in the United States. It gave him the freedom to use a borrowed telephone and make sure there would be no record on the monthly bill of what number had been called. He knew, sadly, that he would never be able to get Remo to use the system. It required remembering numbers, and Remo had no ability and even less desire to remember anything. It had taken him five years to learn the 800 area code number he now used, and Smith thought it was better to leave things alone.

He dialed CURE's local number. The telephone buzzed, and then there was silence as the computers activated the telephone line. They made no sound, and Smith knew he had exactly fifteen seconds to press in his personal identification code before the line went dead.

He held the small round unit over the telephone mouthpiece and depressed the buttons M-C-3-1-9. There was an answering beep through the earpiece. The computer had received the code and was awaiting Smith's instructions.

He tapped out on the small hand-held sender: "LATEST REPORT ON INTERCEPTED TRANSMISSIONS."

He could feel the unit in his hand whir as different electronic circuits were being triggered, then a small sheet of heat-sensitive paper emerged from one end of the unit. When the whirring stopped, he read it.

"LATEST TRANSMISSION INTERCEPTED AT 6 P.M. READS 'THIS IS B. I WILL KILL PRESIDENT IMMEDIATELY UPON HIS RETURN.' "

B? Smith thought. But B was dead. Robin Feldmar, Birdie, had been dead several hours before 6 P.M.

He tapped into the telephone: "ASSUMED B WAS ROBIN FELDMAR. FELDMAR DIED AT 4 P.M. TODAY. CONCLUSION?"

The machine responded instantly: "CONCLUSION, FELDMAR NOT B. B HAS PERSONAL ACCESS TO COMPUTER MESSAGE SYSTEM. B SENT MESSAGE PERSONALLY."

Smith asked: "COULD MAIN COMPUTER SYSTEM BE LOCATED AT DU LAC COLLEGE, MINNESOTA?"

The machine waited several minutes before responding.

"AFFIRMATIVE. CONCLUSION CHECKED. COMPUTER IS AT DU LAC. CAN BE REACHED FROM ANYWHERE BY TELEPHONE HOOKUP."

Smith asked: "WHO ARE RECIPIENTS OF B'S MESSAGES?"

The computer responsed: "NOW CHECKING POTENTIAL HOOKUPS OF DU LAC COMPUTER WITH OTHER MAJOR SYSTEMS."

Smith asked: "HOW LONG WILL IT TAKE?"

The answer: "THREE HOURS."

"DO IT FASTER," Smith wrote.

"THREE HOURS," the computer stubbornly replied.

Smith thought for a moment, then tapped on the machine's keyboard: "CAN YOU PLANT MESSAGE INTO DU LAC SYSTEM BY OVERRIDE?"

"YES."

Smith tapped: "PLANT THIS INFORMATION. THE TRAITOR INSIDE EARTH GOODNESS SOCIETY IS HARRY SMITH. A NEW EMPLOYEE."

"WILL DO AS SOON AS THIS CIRCUIT IS CLEARED," the computer replied.

"OUT. M-C-3-1-9," Smith typed and even as he depressed the last digit, the telephone went dead as the computer cut the connection.

He threw the message paper into the wastebasket. Already its edges were turning dark, and in no more than a minute, the paper would turn totally black. A minute after that, it would disintegrate into powder.

Smith put his telephone device back into his briefcase and carried it over to the couch. He took out his revolver, then locked the case, put it on a chair, and covered it with his suit jacket. He put the gun on the floor under the sofa, then lay down to rest.

The die was cast. In a few hours or a few minutes, the assassin inside Earth Goodness would know Smith was an enemy and would be coming for him. And Smith would know in three hours who the assassins were working for. Who wanted the president dead.

He felt a tingle at the base of his spine. There was danger ahead of him. He knew that, but he felt the excitement of the doer. He could take care of the danger, and he could take care of the threat to the president, and, yes, he could take care of the threat to Mildred Pensoitte.

The thought of the Englishwoman flashed, unbidden, into his mind. Lying in her bed, the skin of her throat creamy white in the dim light of the reading lamp, her arms extended to him in invitation, a smile on her face. He had never had cause before to question or to criticize the stern New England upbringing that had made him who and what he was: a hard, unyielding, narrow man with an overdeveloped sense of duty and obligation, but if he were ever to question it, it would have been now.

The feel of the rough sofa through his shirt made him think how sleek and inviting were the sheets on Mildred Pensoitte's bed. They would be not be bumpy as this sofa was; her bed would be smooth and slippery . . . her body too.

No. Stop.

With an effort of will, he forced her out of his thoughts and reached a hand over his head, turned off the lamp by the side of the sofa, and two minutes later was asleep.

Chapter Twenty-Five

They buried Emrys near the cave. H'si T'ang took the arrangement of pine, bamboo, and plum blossoms from the entrance and placed them on the Welshman's grave. No one spoke until Griffith gave a small cry, weaving where he stood.

"Danger." He spoke softly, his eyes fixed on the sky above.

H'si T'ang raised his hands and then tasted his fingers. "He speaks the truth. There is death in the sky."

"Get inside," Remo said. "Hurry."

Griffith pointed to a cloud bank in the distance. It moved toward them at tremendous speed, changing color from gray to black to brick red as it rolled forward, blanketing the sky. "We will not be safe inside," the boy said.

At that moment, a shaft of lightning ripped through the red clouds and struck the cave, blasting a hole into the side of the hill where it stood. Fragments of clay pots flew out of the entrance, along with burnt shards of the grass matting that coated the floor.

It began to hail. The stabbing pellets hurt Remo.

Hail? Now? It was as senseless an occurrence as the rolling red sky. He forced himself to concentrate. *There was no hail.* It was the Dutchman. If he could understand that, he would be safe from the visions. But what about the others?

Griffith covered his head. Chiun carefully led H'si T'ang behind a large boulder and went to the boy. Jilda looked up, stunned, cupping her hands in front of her. They filled with small stones. One struck her wrist, scraping off the skin. Dots of blood appeared on her arms. She threw the pebbles to the ground. "Who is this man who makes it rain stones upon us?" she shrieked. Her face was a mass of bruises.

"It's his mind," Remo shouted above the din of falling rock. He tried to cover Jilda with his own body. "There aren't really any stones. Look at me." There was not a mark on his body. "They only exist if you believe they do. Don't trust your eyes. They aren't real, I tell you."

Griffith whimpered. His neck and arms were covered with blood. Chiun, doing all he could to protect the boy, shook his head. There was nothing he could do against an enemy who killed his victims from inside their minds.

"But they do believe," a voice said from near the cave. The Dutchman was standing on the hill over the entrance. He was smiling. Even at a distance, Jilda could see the terrifying power in his electric-blue eyes.

"I have come for Chiun," he said. "Let him fight me now, Chiun alone."

"I cannot fight you," the old man said. "It is against the laws of Sinanju."

"I'll fight you," Remo said.

"You are nothing to me. To kill you will bring me no satisfaction. It must be Chiun." He waved one arm slowly.

The stones disappeared. The sky rolled back. The sun shone.

Silently, while he spoke, Jilda picked up her spear. She hurled it so hard that her feet left the ground.

"Devil,"she muttered as the weapon flew toward him.

The Dutchman's hands moved. The spear shattered into a thousand pieces in midair.

"The girl amuses me," he said. "And she is a beauty. Perhaps she will please me later."

"See if this pleases you, scum," she shouted, taking her ax from her belt.

"Jilda—" Remo reached for the ax. Jilda kicked at him.

"He is mine," she said.

She rushed at the hill, stopping suddenly near the cave. The Dutchman watched her.

"Go ahead. Attack," he said, smiling.

Her breath was labored. She clutched the ax tightly. She turned. Her eyes were frightened, her mouth twisted.

"Jilda?" Remo asked, walking uncertainly toward her.

"Stay away," she hissed. "I can't—I don't know what he's doing." She broke into a run. When she was near Remo, she swung the ax with all her force at Remo's neck.

He leaped out of the way. It had been so close that he had felt the wake of the blade.

"Run!" she shouted. "I cannot stop!" She attacked him again. He struggled with her, but her strength was enormous. She pulled away and swung, screaming, full force at Remo's belly.

He saw the blow coming. At the beginning of the swing, he flattened himself on the ground and rolled toward her, knocking Jilda off her feet. Then, spiraling upward, he kicked the ax away and landed on her hand, hard. He heard the small bones crack, and when she moaned with the pain, he felt as if a hammerblow had been struck into his own gut.

"I couldn't let you go on," he said.

She lay on the ground, curled into a ball. The useless hand stretched in front of her. "I know," she said. She hid her face so that he could not see her tears.

Chiun watched it all in horror. He had not expected the Dutchman's power to be so complete.

The laws of Sinanju had prohibited him from killing the man when he'd had the opportunity. He had obeyed those laws. Now he realized that by letting him live, he had unleashed a beast that would destroy them all. Now it was too late to fight him. The Dutchman was too powerful. Remo had been the only hope, but Remo still did not understand that he was Shiva. He, too, had no chance. There was only one thing left to do.

Chiun walked slowly into the clearing. "It is I you want," he said. "Very well. I understand your power. I cannot fight you, for reasons known only to my village."

"Chiun!" Remo shouted. "What are you saying?"

"Take me. Let the others live."

"Oh, no, you don't," Remo said, joining the old Oriental. "You take him on, you take me, too. You might be able to kill one of us in battle, but not both of us together."

"No," Chiun insisted. "If there were even the smallest hope that we could fight him and live, I would take it. But there is none. You've seen what he can do. I am an old man, and have made my peace. Let me go."

Remo swallowed. He looked up at the Dutchman. "You don't get to him unless you take me first," he said.

"That will be no problem," the Dutchman said. From his perch on the hill, he raised both arms, his fingers curved like the talons of a bird of prey. The blue eyes glowed. From them came a wave of pure energy, as powerful as the shock waves from a nuclear blast.

Remo felt as if the skin on his skull were rolling back with the force. It took all his concentration to remain standing. His shoulders began to shake. His breath came shallowly. He felt a spot in the center of his chest giving way. His heart. His heart was about to burst right out of his body. He wasn't even going to get a chance to fight.

He closed his eyes. No sight, no sound. Nothing remained before him but the gaping hole of the Void.

He thought of Jilda. Her hand would heal in time, even if she couldn't fight anymore. It was just as well. She was awfully beautiful to be a warrior. He only wished he could have met her earlier. It hadn't been enough time. But then, a lifetime wouldn't have been enough time with her.

And Chiun. The pain would be tough on Chiun.

Remo tried to speak, but couldn't. His mind formed the words: *I'm sorry I let you down, Father.*

The pressure receded. Chiun must have heard him. It would soon be over for both of them.

But the Dutchman's force didn't only lessen. It died altogether. With a deep, involuntary breath, Remo opened his eyes. He and Chiun both stood in the shadow of H'si T'ang.

The old Master had stepped in front of them both to absorb the full power of the Dutchman alone. Chiun made a move to stop him, but H'si T'ang held out his hand.

"I can withstand him better than you," the blind man said.

The Dutchman's face contorted.

"He is weakened," Chiun said, amazed.

While the Dutchman focused his concentration on H'si T'ang, Remo ran silently behind the hill and climbed it swiftly. The Dutchman never turned. Using his strongest attack, Remo sent out both legs in a powerful thrust aimed at the Dutchman's spine.

The legs swung through empty air. There was no one on the hill.

Below, Remo saw H'si T'ang clutch at his chest and fall. At the same moment, the Dutchman stepped from behind a bush near the old man.

"A mirage," Remo said, feeling his heart sink. The figure on the hill had been no more than the projection of an image in the Dutchman's mind. He had been standing near them all along.

But something was wrong. Chiun wasn't watching the man coming from the bushes. He was bending over H'si T'ang, massaging the old man's chest.

"Chiun! Behind you!" Remo screamed.

But the Dutchman had already prepared his blow by then, and even though Chiun readied himself in an instant, he was too late. The Dutchman's hands moved like lightning, striking two fierce slices into Chiun's abdomen. The old Oriental seemed to fly through the air, arms windmilling. His face registered pain for the first time Remo could remember. He landed face down in the sandy grass.

The thin old body didn't move. Chiun's gown was twisted between his legs, making him look like a strange little doll that someone had discarded. His feet showed.

"Chiun?" Remo whispered, unable to believe the sight before his eyes. Jilda, clutching her broken hand in the other, her face swollen from the rocks that had struck it, screamed in terror. The boy, Griffith, knelt by H'si T'ang, whose legs twitched weakly.

The Dutchman looked expectantly at the ground, then the sky. He examined his hands. He was speaking. A gust of wind carried his words to Remo on the hill.

"It is the same," he said, sounding surprised. "There is no peace from killing him. You promised me rest, Nuihc. What of your promise?"

And far away from all of them lay Chiun, lifeless and

still. The old man was dead. It had never before occurred to Remo that Chiun would die.

Inside him grew a sadness so deep that his body could not contain it. Remo lifted his head and wailed like a man who had saved all the frights and tears of his life for one moment.

"My father," he called.

It was time to fight the Dutchman. Alone. He walked down the hill to meet his opponent. His last opponent, most likely. If the Dutchman's power was greater than Chiun's, it surely surpassed his own.

The thoughts passed through his mind like wisps of air. It didn't matter. He cast one more glance at Chiun.

There was so little left to lose now.

Chapter Twenty-Six

Smith slid into consciousness. He was not alone. There had been some kind of a light flashing, and now there was someone in the room, and his hand started to move down toward the revolver, which he had hidden under the sofa.

But his hand stopped when it met something smooth and soft. It was fabric—satin—and it was draped over the legs of Mildred Pensoitte.

"Mildred?"

"Shhhhh."

"Are you all right?" he asked.

"Shhhhhh," she whispered again. He tried to raise himself to a sitting position, but she put her hands on his shoulders and pushed him back onto the sofa.

How long had he been asleep? He glanced at his watch. Less than two hours.

Mildred Pensoitte was wearing a long white satin robe that flickered eerily in the moonlight. Her hands were still on his shoulders, and then she moved closer to him, and then she was straddling him, looking down at him, one leg on each side of his waist.

"Did you think you were going to survive the night?" she asked. He could see her smiling in the faint light that the bright moon reflected into the room.

"Please, Mildred. We can't."

"We must," she said.

She reached down to open his shirt buttons. The moon emerged from behind a cloud and he saw her smile again, but it was a different smile now. It was a hard and cold smile, and there was no warmth in it. It was a smile he had seen before, many years ago, and she said again, "We must," and her hand went to a pocket in her satin robe, and in the moonlight he saw a knife glinting in her hand. As she plunged the knife down toward his throat, Smith spun and rolled and dumped her off him onto the floor.

Smith sprang to his feet, grabbed his revolver, and ran across the room to flick on the light switch.

Mildred Pensiotte was on the floor, her knife still in her hand. The white robe was open, and her breasts were exposed.

"Is that the knife you used to kill Robin Feldmar?" Smith asked.

"Yes." Her voice was chilled as ice.

"Why?" Smith asked.

"Because she would have talked. She talked too much. You can have cranks around when you're starting up and all you're doing is talking. But when you get to action, to doing things, those people are dangerous."

"The revolution eats its own children," Smith said softly. "When did you know it was me?"

"A few minutes ago. I called the computer at Du Lac College. It said that you were the spy in Earth Goodness. What are you? CIA? FBI?"

"None of those," Smith said. "Why do they call you B?"

"You know about that," she said with some surprise.

"I should have known. From the moment you came aboard, all we've had is confusion and death and disorder. I should have known it was you."

"Why do they call you B?"

"Bunny. A childhood nickname," she said.

"I thought it meant Birdie. Feldmar," he said.

She shook her head. "She was too stupid to be real. With her antics, marching around those lunatic college children, as if they counted for anything."

She rose to her feet. The robe hung open over her opulent body. She dropped the knife in front of her on the floor and extended her arms toward Smith and came across the room to him.

"We can still have it," she said. "We can have it all."

She smiled, and Smith remembered where he had seen that smile. It was in a French farmhouse, and the girl who had smiled had been responsible for the deaths of fifteen of Smith's men. She had smiled too, and Smith had killed her.

He concentrated on the smile, and he hesitated, and Mildred Pensiotte's smile grew wider. Her hands reached to her waist and pulled her robe open wide.

The smile. The dead weren't smiling. They were in St. Martin's and Washington, and they would be all over if this woman had her way.

She smiled again and Smith smiled back.

And fired his revolver.

"Good-bye, Bunny," Smith said.

Back in his mid-town office at Earth Goodness, Inc., Smith again called the Folcroft computers.

He punched his code into the triggering device, then signaled: "WHAT HOOKUP OF DU LAC COMPUTER WITH OTHER MAJOR SYSTEMS?"

The computer reported back: "SYSTEM HOOKED BY MICROWAVE TO CUBAN OFFICE OF KGB."

Smith paused a moment. The Russians had been behind the plot to kill the president. Mildred Pensiotte and, to a lesser degree, Robin Feldmar, had been Soviet plants, spies working in this country to help overthrow it. The awful thing, he thought, was probably that no one would ever know.

He directed the computers: "VACUUM DU LAC," then entered his code and hung up. In moments, he knew, the giant Folcroft computers would be sweeping clean all the memories from the Du Lac computers. Who knew what might be in those files? There might be some little bit of information that one day might provide him with leverage he might not otherwise have in dealing with America's enemies.

He looked up a number in his wallet and dialed.

The secretary of the interior answered the telephone himself. He was sleepy, and his voice was thick with exhaustion.

"Yes?" he said.

"This is Smith. Tell the president it's safe to come home."

He hung up and thought again of Remo and Chiun. There they were, off, gallivanting around on a vacation, leaving it to him to protect America and the free world. They'd hear about it when they got back. They'd hear what a hell of a nerve they had leaving all the dirty work for Smith while they were off disporting themselves.

Chapter Twenty-Seven

The Dutchman groveled on all fours, muttering. "You promised me, Nuihc. You said . . . you said . . ."

Remo approached him like a man whose soul had died. His eyes were blank, his face expressionless. He stopped in front of the Dutchman and kicked him in the throat.

The Dutchman rolled over, startled.

"Get up," Remo said. Before the Dutchman could rise, Remo kicked him again.

"I have no quarrel with you," the blond man rasped.

"Think of one." Remo slapped him flat across the face.

The Dutchman stood to full height. "Don't do this," he warned. "I am trying—"

Remo sent two jabs to the man's belly. "I don't care if you fight me or not," Remo said quietly. "As long as I hurt you." He slammed an elbow into the man's hip, which sent the Dutchman sprawling.

A mist appeared instantly, settling over the landscape. The hills softened into pastel domes, like melting ice cream.

"And you can save the artwork, too. I know where you are."

"Do you?" the voice came from behind him. Remo turned. Five identical figures, all the Dutchman, peered at him through the fog. "Where am I, Remo?"

The five figures disappeared. Another materialized beside him. Remo swung at it. It faded into smoke. "Or am I everywhere?" In a flash of light, the ice cream mountaintops glowed in phosphorescent colors. On the peak of each stood the Dutchman, hundreds of him, like tiny paper cutouts.

Remo stood still and watched. There were no birds in the sky. The fields were quiet. The Dutchman was *real,* he told himself, no matter how many figments of himself he could produce. And that one real being moved on two legs like anyone else. Remo shifted his eyes out of focus and concentrated entirely on his peripheral vision.

Through the fog, to the right of Remo, a figure ran, crouching. He moved swiftly and silently, using all the skill of a lifetime of training. He climbed the highest hill in the area, stopping behind a large dead tree.

Another figment appeared directly beside Remo, prepared to strike. Remo clenched his jaws and walked through it. He had things to do now.

Kiree . . . Kiree and Ancion. They had both known things that were new to Remo. Things that could help him against an enemy more powerful than himself. If he could just remember. He stooped to gather two handfuls of grass and a rock the size of a baseball. He stuffed the rock inside his belt and began to rub the blades of grass.

Lightning flashed across the sky. A high wind gusted out of nowhere. Remo ignored them, and was left untouched. He concentrated on disintegrating the grass, as Kiree had done, his hands moving so fast that the moisture in the blades evaporated instantly. He spat, slapping his hands together in rhythm.

He had to take the Dutchman by surprise. No matter

how fast he ran, the Dutchman would see him coming in plenty of time to perform one of his tricks. Remo knew that the changes in weather and the constantly shifting landscape were visual lies, but the Dutchman could be subtle. What if he made Jilda burst into flame? Or caused the top of Griffith's head to explode like a firecracker? They weren't invulnerable to his ugly games. No, this contest had to be between Remo and the Dutchman, one on one. Remo didn't expect to win, but he wasn't about to make anyone else take the loss with him.

"Fool," the Dutchman sneered. "You waste my time."

Remo spat into his hands again. The pulp was almost the right consistency. He pulled his hands away, and like taffy, the wire-thin fibers formed. He worked quickly, weaving the fine, transparent net around the rock. His hands were moving too fast to see.

"Your skin is burning," the Dutchman insinuated. "Your eyes are dry and withering. Blisters cover your body."

"Go eat a toad." It was ready. With one swing, Remo wound the net around a tree and swung up. The second propelled him to a boulder. On the third orbit of the net, he flew toward the crag where the Dutchman waited and landed with both feet in the blond man's chest.

"Thanks, guys," he said to the spirits of Ancion and Kiree. Somewhere, he felt, from some unknown vantage point, they were watching.

With a whoosh of air from his lungs, the Dutchman fell down the hill. At its base, he righted himself awkwardly and ran. Remo followed him. The ground was soft and covered with holes. The snakes, Remo remembered. Watch it. He can make them come out your ears if he wants to.

But the Dutchman had no hallucination waiting. He stood beside an open pit, absorbed in its swarming interior. Remo approached, standing across the wide hole from him. The pit contained the skeletons of four men, picked clean by scavengers. They were loosely draped in rags that had once been uniforms of some sort. Over them crawled more snakes than Remo had ever seen in one place.

The two men circled the pit. The Dutchman's eyes were pale and lucid, the maniacal fire in them gone. Instead, they held a look of bewilderment as he searched Remo's face.

"Who are you?" the Dutchman asked. It was a plea.

Strange music came to Remo on the wind. Faint but insistent, the dissonant melody was the same as the strains he had heard when he first came to the shores of Sinanju with Jilda and the others. It had filled him with terror then, but now the music carried no more fear than a passing breeze. It was the Dutchman's music, but devoid of the Dutchman's power.

He feeds on fear, Remo thought. When he had stopped caring whether he lived or died, he had lost his fear of the Dutchman. And without the fear, he was no longer a victim.

The music swelled again, and suddenly Remo recognized it for what it was. It had sounded oddly familiar the first time he heard it, but didn't understand why. Now he knew. He had heard the same notes long ago, in a small boat setting off to carry him to the first stop in the Master's Trial. It was Chiun's music, note for note, only distorted, a perversion of the songs of Sinanju.

And as he watched the Dutchman standing in mirror image of himself, he understood the music's meaning. "I am you," he answered.

Yin and yang.

Light and shadow, good and evil, Remo and the Dutchman were opposite sides of the same being. They were born of the same traditions, both white men taken out of their societies and created anew in the ways of Sinanju. They both claimed Masters of the discipline as their fathers.

Only fate had kept them apart for so long. Now, together, they formed a whole that could only end in destruction.

"If I kill you, I will die," the Dutchman said, sounding almost relieved. "It was you all along. I have been seeking the wrong man."

"You killed him."

"As I must kill you," the Dutchman said.

In one perfect spiral leap, he crossed the pit and delivered a blow to Remo's chest. His ribs broke under the impact. He tried to right himself, but the Dutchman was too fast. Remo felt a shattering pain in his kneecap that sent him flying toward a boulder. He landed on his shoulder.

The Dutchman kicked him off the rock. "It can't be done quickly," he said softly. "I've waited too long. The victory must be complete."

He stepped back. Remo stirred. The Dutchman crushed his elbow with his heel. The pain flooded over Remo like a wave. His vision receded to a wash of color: black, red, iridescent blue. . . .

"You will hear me now, and obey," the Dutchman commanded.

It was the fear. *Stop the fear in yourself, and his power will vanish.*

But he was afraid. No man had ever attacked him so fast. No man had ever beaten him so completely. The Dutchman was better than he was, better than anyone. In the Master's Trial, the Dutchman would have conquered the world.

"Feel the knives in your legs, Remo."

Remo screamed with the pain. Thousands of blades were suddenly embedded in his skin, cutting to the bone.

"They are in your hands now, your arms. . . ."

He felt his palms flatten. The knives, slicing his flesh by inches, moved up his arms. Each thrust was an agony.

Each knife brought him closer to the welcome numbness of death.

"Oh, Chiun," Remo whispered.

His eyes fluttered open. In the distance were three moving figures, barely visible. Remo tried to concentrate on them to lessen the pain. He was going to die, but Chiun had once told him that death did not have to be painful. "Take yourself out of the pain," Chiun had said. Chiun . . .

It was Chiun. The old man was alive, walking between Jilda and the boy. The three of them stopped beside H'si T'ang, seated on the ground. Chiun picked his teacher up and moved in a wooden gait toward the cave. As he walked, Chiun turned his head right and left, searching.

"I am here, Father," Remo said, too weak to be heard. "I, too, am still alive."

Then, from a place deep in his soul, another voice spoke:

I am created Shiva, the Destroyer; death, the shatterer of worlds;

The dead night tiger made whole by the Master of Sinanju.

Remo rose. He was covered with the wounds he had permitted in his fear, but the knives were gone.

The Dutchman regarded him, puzzled. When he spoke, his voice was full of false confidence. "You can't fight me now. Look at you."

Blood dripped off Remo's hands in pools. But the Dutchman's eyes were afraid. He prepared to strike.

Remo attacked before the Dutchman's hands could reach him. Through the pain, despite his broken bones and the blood that covered him, he struck three times, three perfect blows. The Dutchman fell, screaming, into the snake pit.

Remo watched the sinuous creatures slither over the stunned man who sat sprawled among the bones of the dead. The Dutchman made no attempt to move. Instead, a thin half-smile spread over his face. A drop of bright blood appeared at the corners of the Dutchman's lips and swelled to a stream.

"It is here at last," he said weakly. "The peace I have sought all my life. It is a great comfort."

Remo wanted to turn away, but he was unable. His eyes were locked into the Dutchman's. He felt himself weakening, warming with a flood of quiet resignation. Involuntarily, he dropped to his knees.

"Don't you see?" the Dutchman said. "We are the same being. Not men, but something else." He grimaced with a stab of pain. Remo felt it, too, at the same moment. "We grow closer now, in death. I am sorry to take you with me, but it is the only way. With you, I can finally find rest."

Remo nodded slowly. He understood the prophecy.

The Other will join with his own kind. Yin and yang will be one in the spring of the Year of the Tiger.

The Dutchman had to die, it was necessary. And when he died, Remo would have to die with him. Yin and yang, light and darkness, life and death, together. It was the prophecy come to fruition.

He arranged himself in full lotus before the pit and waited, his spirit entwined with the Dutchman's, to enter the Void.

Chapter Twenty-Eight

Someone slapped his face. The jolt pulled Remo out of his deep trance. Jilda, bruised and cut, was kneeling close to him.

"I've looked everywhere for you," she said, kissing him. "You'll be all right now. Put your arm around my shoulder." Gently she tried to lift him up.

Still stuporous, he picked up Jilda's rag-bandaged hand. "I'm sorry," he said.

"You had no choice. It is forgotten."

He pulled away from her. "Chiun. He's alive. I saw him."

"Yes. He lost consciousness, but he is well now."

"And H'si T'ang?"

"Chiun does not think the Venerable One will recover. It is his heart."

Remo fumbled to his knees. "Wait," he said. In the pit, the Dutchman was still sitting, motionless, his eyes frozen into a stare. The snakes were gone.

"But he couldn't have died without me." He made a move to enter the pit.

Jilda pulled him back. "Come, Remo. You have lost so much blood. What did he do to you?"

"Don't . . . remember," Remo faltered. "But he shouldn't be . . . shouldn't be . . ." Confused, he followed her back to the cave.

Chiun was pale, but his eyes sparkled when he saw Remo. H'si T'ang lay on his back in a space cleared of the rubble from the Dutchman's lightning attack. The floor, stripped of its straw matting, was bare and cold, but Chiun had laid one of his brocade robes beneath his old teacher. Griffith knelt beside the old man, who smiled.

"Your return is welcome, son of my son."

"Thank you, Master," Remo said.

"There is no danger in the air. Has the Other gone to the Void?"

"Yes. I think so."

"You think?" Chiun asked.

Something was wrong. The knowledge that Remo and the Dutchman would die together was not a figment of anyone's imagination. They had both known it as surely as they knew the sun rose in the east. Yet Remo was still alive.

"He's dead," Remo said.

"Remo," H'si T'ang said, his ancient hands groping forward to touch him. "You are badly hurt."

"Not too badly. I can walk."

The old man frowned. "No power," he said. "I cannot heal you anymore."

"That's all right," Remo said, composing H'si T'ang's hands in front of him.

"But you are too weak . . ."

"I'm all right. You're the one who needs to get better. You saved us both."

"Thank you," H'si T'ang said gently, "but only the young wish to live forever. I am but one step from the

Void. It will be an easy step, one I am eager to take.'' He smiled. ''Besides, it is our belief that a man's spirit does not enter the Void with him. It is passed to another, and thus lives forever.''

Remo remembered Kiree, who had fought so bravely in the hills of Africa. ''I hope that's true,'' he said.

The old man coughed. His breath came in spasms, swelling the features of his face. ''Chiun?'' He raised his trembling hands. ''Chiun, my son.''

H'si T'ang struggled to speak, but no words came. In time, the withered hands stilled, and the ancient parchment-skinned face sank into blankness.

After several moments, Chiun spoke, in a quavering voice, the benediction for the death of his teacher: ''And so it came to pass that in the spring of the Year of the Tiger did the Master of Sinanju die, as was foretold in the legends of ancient times. And thus did the Master become one with the spirit of all things.''

Jilda led Griffith away. ''What was H'si T'ang trying to say?'' the boy whispered. Remo left, too, to leave Chiun alone with his grief.

They walked slowly back toward the pit where Remo had left the Dutchman. ''He's got to be dead,'' Remo said, hurrying.

''Of course he is,'' Jilda answered. ''I saw him myself. There's no need to go back to that awful place.''

Oh, yes there is, a nagging voice inside him said. He ran ahead, stopping at the edge of the pit.

''Well, we have to do something with ourselves, I suppose,'' Jilda said.

''I want to see the snakes,'' Griffith said.

''The snakes were gone. There was only . . . only . . .'' She walked around the open pit. There was nothing inside but some scattered bones.

''He *is* dead,'' Remo insisted, furious. He stared at the

bones as if he believed he could make the Dutchman materialize out of them.

Jilda lowered herself into the hole and prodded the earth with her toes.

"This is another trick of his," Remo said. His voice was harsh and rasping. He clenched and unclenched his fists, opening the congealed wounds in his hands. "He's there. We just can't see him. He's—"

"He is gone, Remo," Jilda said. She uncovered a hole beneath a large, flat rock. The hole was big enough for a man to crawl through. "That's where he went."

"No!" Remo shouted, shaking with anger. He vaulted into the pit and worked his way through the freshly dug tunnel as fast as he could. "No!" he called from inside the earth. "No!" at the tunnel's mouth beside the ocean's rocky shore.

There was nothing ahead of him but a clear expanse of blue water.

It had been a waste, all of it—H'si T'ang's death, Jilda's suffering, Chiun's humiliation, his own efforts. He had failed them all. The Dutchman was still alive and would spread his poison around the world. He had lived because Remo had been too weak to die with him.

"Why didn't you take us both?" he screamed into the empty, indifferent sea.

There was no answer.

Chapter Twenty-Nine

Remo took a long time returning to the cave. Inside, Chiun, Jilda and Griffith kept watch over the body of H'si T'ang. A single candle lit the features of the dead man.

The three of them watched Remo enter, his shoulders stooped. "He's gone," he said. He walked to the far corner of the cave and sat on a heap of fallen rock.

Chiun and Jilda were silent. Only Griffith stood up. He walked to the center of the cave, to a spot where the afternoon sun poured through a hole in the rock. The light illuminated his dirty face. Without speaking, he raised his battered arms to shoulder level, palms up. In the sunlight, his wounds seemed to disappear.

Remo rose slowly. They *had* disappeared. The boy's skin was as smooth and brown as seasoned wood.

"How in the—"

The boy silenced him with a look. His eyes were glassy and faraway, and carried in them an innate authority far beyond his years. Chiun motioned Remo abstractedly to sit down.

"My spirit do I bequeath to this child," Griffith began in a voice unrecognizable as his own.

"H'si T'ang," Chiun whispered. "He lives."

"Only my spirit lives, the essence of what my life has been. The boy's soul and mind shall always remain his own. My knowledge only is added to what he already possesses. He has always had the Sight in some measure, and so will use the gift wisely and well, if he is taught correctly. Tell him, when I have finished, of his legacy, for he cannot hear my words, and will be afraid of his powers. I beg you, do not permit him to grow like the Dutchman, fearful and lonely."

"I will not," Jilda said.

"My fierce and beautiful warrior," the voice inside the boy said to the woman. "You have risked much, given much. Your courage has not gone unnoticed. Be strong, Jilda, for just a short time longer. Much will depend on you."

She nodded, too overcome to speak.

Griffith turned his strange, unseeing eyes on Chiun. "You called me your father, and that I am. For though you are not my natural son, you have pleased me beyond my expectations. For you, Chiun, are the greatest of all the Masters of Sinanju who have walked this earth. It was for this reason that the charge of Shiva was placed upon you."

Chiun's eyes welled.

"It was this that I tried to tell you while I was still among you. But I was weak, and the Void called irresistibly to me. And so I tell you now. I could not have found a better son if I searched all the world until the end of time."

"Father," Chiun whispered.

Finally, the boy turned to Remo. "And you. Do you yet know who you are? What you are?"

Remo turned his head. "I've failed," he said.

"You have failed only to alter the course of destiny." H'si T'ang spoke angrily through the boy. "Is your arrogance such that you believe you can control even the forces of the universe?''

"What? No," Remo stammered. "No. It's nothing like that. Only—"

"Then you must realize that even Shiva does not possess the power to take a life before its appointed time to die."

Before its—"

"The Other lives because you must live. Yin and yang, light and darkness. Both must exist. There is a great destiny before you, Remo. Have the courage to fulfill it."

"I . . . I . . ." The boy's eyes seemed to bore into his very soul. He fell silent.

Griffith's face grew gentle. He stepped close to Remo. "You have fought well, son of my son." He touched Remo's hand. The knife wounds disappeared.

Remo examined himself in amazement as the boy went to Jilda and caressed her face. The bruises and cuts healed instantly. He unwrapped the bandage around her hand. Beneath it the flesh and bones and skin were once again perfect.

"And now I speak my last words to you all, for I shall not appear again," Griffith said feverishly. "Go back to your lands in peace. Keep in your hearts the balance of the universe. Live your lives in honor and wisdom."

Then the boy sank to the floor, unconscious.

Jilda cradled him in her arms. "You will not fear this gift you have, little one," she said. "The Lady of the Lake will see to that."

Chapter Thirty

Since the start of the Master's Trial, spring in Sinanju had changed almost imperceptibly into summer. Crickets and tree frogs called endlessly through the warm night, and the air was fragrant with the scent of ripening plum blossoms.

Remo lay with Jilda on a bank of cool moss. In the distance was music. Chiun was playing his belled instrument near the graves of H'si T'ang and Emrys. The melody was the same one he had played for Remo's Ritual of Parting so long ago, before the Dutchman came. Now its notes rang again, serene and beautiful, in another ritual of parting.

Remo kissed the smooth skin at the nape of Jilda's neck, still flushed with passion. Making love, even with Jilda, had never been so good as this last time, beneath the open night sky. There had been an urgency about her caresses, a hunger that she had needed him to satisfy. "You make me very happy," he said, lifting her chin. Her eyes were filled with tears. "What's the matter?"

"Nothing," she said quickly, drawing her hand over her

face. "I am happy, too. I never thought I would find you. I mean, someone like you," she added.

"No. Not someone like me or someone like you. You, the original, and me. That's the only combination that works."

Jilda looked up at the stars. Gullikona, the Golden Lady of the sky, was burning in all her glory. "Sometimes I feel as if the love we have was meant to be," she said softly. "Like the princess and the warrior of the legend."

"They don't even come close," Remo said. He looked out to sea. "Jilda, the submarine from the States is due in tomorrow."

"No!" She held him fiercely. "We will not speak of tomorrow."

"Why not?"

"I will not cross the sea in an iron fish," she said. "I have built my own boat. It is hidden near the shore."

Remo laughed. "Ever the stubborn barbarian," he said. "Look, the sub's perfectly safe, and it'll save us weeks of travel. Just trust me, okay? We'll set Griffith up with some relatives, and then—"

"I will remain with Griffith." She held his glance for a moment, then turned away. "He is an exceptional boy. His upbringing cannot be entrusted to people who do not understand him."

"Spoken like a true mother."

"It was my promise to H'si T'ang. He was a wise man. We would all do well to listen to what he has said."

"Meaning what?"

Jilda bit her lip. "It will only be necessary to spend a few years with Griffith. After he is grown, I will return to Lakluun. Where I belong."

"Hey," Remo said gently. "Is that what's bothering you?" He stroked her hair. "You don't have to change your life for me. I love you, funnyface, remember?" He tweaked her nose. Her green eyes changed to blue and then gray and back to green again, like the shifting hues of an ocean. "God, I'll never get used to those," he said.

"Remo . . ."

"Shhh. Listen to me. If you've got to stay in Wales, I'll stay with you. We'll raise Griffith together. No problem. I've always wanted a kid, anyway."

His thoughts ran to their life together in the green hills of Emrys's valley. The three of them in the Forest Primeval. Me Tarzan, you Jilda. His face flushed, and his hands grew cold. He liked the feeling. He liked it very much. "I'll build you a nice little house," he said eagerly. "With a picket fence around it. No fair spearing any animals on the fence. And we'll plant some flowers around the front, just like in the movies."

"Oh, Remo—"

"And when Griffith's good and sick of us telling him how to run his life, we'll take off in one of your crazy canoes and row ourselves to Viking Land, and swim in ice water and swill mead with the boys—"

"Stop!" She didn't bother to check her tears now.

"I don't understand," Remo said quietly. "I'm asking you to marry me." He stared at her in bewilderment. "Don't you . . . I mean, I thought you wanted . . ."

"Above all things, I wish to spend my life with you. But the sacrifice . . . the sacrifice will be too great."

"There wouldn't have to be any sacrifice, I'm telling you."

"Not for me, Remo. For you."

"For me? You've got to be kidding. I've spent my whole life in orphanages and army barracks and motel rooms. A cottage in Wales'll seem like a castle as far as I'm concerned."

"It is not the *place*," she said. "What you would be

giving up is something inside you, something so rare that the sages among your people have waited for millennia to see it.'' She took Remo's hand in hers. ''You listened to the words of H'si T'ang. You have a great destiny before you. You cannot abandon that for something as selfish, as small as—''

''Small?'' Remo shouted, rising to his feet. ''*Small*? Is that all you think of us?'' He picked up a rock and threw it so hard that it whistled. ''Damn it, I don't want a 'great destiny.' I want to be happy, and for the first time in my life, I am. I want this. I want . . .'' His voice cracked. ''You.''

It was a long time before Jilda spoke. ''That is why I must leave you,'' she said quietly.

The song of the tree frogs, combined with Chiun's distant melody, seemed to fill the world.

''*What*?'' he whispered.

She didn't answer. She gathered her things and dressed quickly, pretending not to see Remo standing beneath the plum tree. Her vision blurred. ''Good-bye,'' she said.

He raced to stop her. ''Tell me you don't love me.''

''Remo—''

He shook her. ''You can't believe in that prophecy crap any more than I do. I'll let you go if you want to go, but not because of any bullshit legend. Just tell me you don't want me, and I'll leave you alone. That's all I'll accept. Otherwise, you're stuck with me. For better or worse.''

''Remo, I can't. It's not fair of you.''

''Tell me! Do you love me or not?''

The moon shifted. Her face, more beautiful than Remo had ever seen it, was bathed in pearlescent light.

''Good,'' Remo said. ''For a minute, I thought—''

''I don't love you.'' She pulled away from him abruptly. Remo exhaled as if someone had kicked him in the belly.

She backed away into the shadows. ''I don't love you.

Now go to your own world, your own life, for everyone's sake. Go, be what you were meant to be.''

She turned and ran. Remo watched her, too stunned to move. A sudden gust of wind blew a shower of blossoms from the plum tree to the ground. In a moment she was gone.

Chapter Thirty-One

Smith had finished scanning the Du Lac College computer tapes, and he finally went home for dinner. He had been gone for two weeks.

Irma was cooking.

"Hello, dear," she said, without turning from the stove.

"Hello, Irma," he said and gave her a peck on the cheek. She did not ask where he had been or what he had been doing. He was home, safely, and that was all that counted.

Dinner was burned pot roast and potatoes, cooked rock-hard in the center.

Dessert was rice pudding. Smith had never liked rice pudding, but he had been trained to finish what was put in front of him, and so Irma never knew. Thirty years ago, his mother had told Irma that he didn't like rice pudding.

Irma kept serving it. She was sure it was his mother's rice pudding that Harold Smith didn't like.

Chapter Thirty-Two

Remo never left his cabin on the long submarine ride back to the United States. It was not until Chiun, still wearing the white robes of mourning, told him that it was time to leave that Remo even moved from his bunk.

It was dark outside when the two of them walked down the dock toward a waiting automobile.

"I'll walk," Remo said.

Chiun nodded, dismissing the car.

"You don't have to come with me."

"You have been alone long enough," the old man said. His white robes billowed in the summer breeze. Remo felt a pang of conscience.

"I'm sorry about H'si T'ang," he said.

"My father lived a full life, and his spirit continues through the boy. I cannot ask for more."

The moon was bright, and the sky was ablaze with stars. Remo kept his head down. He never wanted to look at stars again.

After a long silence, Chiun spoke softly. "I have been giving thought to many things," he said. "To legends and traditions and the continuity of life. It is good that the Master's Trial has been abolished.''

Remo spat.

''Was it so distasteful to you? Did you learn nothing from it?''

''Oh, I learned, all right,'' Remo said bitterly. ''I learned a whole lot. ''

''Such as?''

''Such as I should have stuck to bashing heads for Smitty. That's about all I'm good for.''

''I see,'' Chiun said. ''Then you found nothing of value in Ancion's sense of fairness? Or Kiree's humility? Or Emrys's courage?''

Remo looked over to him. ''Yeah, I guess so. They were good. Better than me, I think, in a lot of ways.''

''And the Dutchman?''

Remo hung his head. ''He was a lot better.''

''Was he?''

Remo knew what he meant. ''Little Father, is there such a thing as . . . well, opposite personalities in people? I mean, different parts of the same person, only in two different bodies?''

''The principle of yin and yang holds true for all things.''

''But . . .''

''He is part of you,'' Chiun said.

Remo made a noise. ''That stuff doesn't make any sense to me.''

''If the force of the universe were so simple as to be understandable to all, life would be a very uninteresting experience.''

''It's been too interesting for my taste. Anyway, he's gone now. I can live with him as long as he stays away from me.''

Chiun shrugged. "Perhaps he will, perhaps not. If he ever returns, it will be different because now you know who you are. And Jilda?"

"What about her?" He worked to keep his voice natural.

"Have you learned from her as well?"

"What's anybody learn from women? They come and they go. They're all the same in the dark."

"That is unworthy of you," Chiun snapped. "Jilda was the equal of any man in the Master's Trial."

"She was all right," Remo said dismissively. "She had weird eyes."

"She possessed great courage. Greater than you know."

"What's that supposed to mean?" Remo said angrily. "That she doesn't lead a guy on? Well, that's true. Jilda and her trusty ax, hacking her way to independence. She can write a book. *The One-Minute Way to Dump on Men*. The women's libbers would love her."

"She carries your child."

Remo stopped dead. "She told you that?"

"She did not have to. I have seen pregnant women before."

"Well, I've seen her, too," Remo said skeptically. "And at closer quarters than you."

"It was her manner, not her body. Ever since you arrived in Sinanju with her, I have observed her. It is true. I thought you would leave with her."

Remo stepped back, his face pale. "I would have. I wanted . . . I've got to get back to her." He turned back toward the dock.

"No, my son," Chiun said. "It is not what she wishes. When she came back to the cave to fetch Griffith, I confronted her with my knowledge. She made me promise never to tell you."

Remo was trembling. "Why?"

"Because she understands more than you what you must do. What you will become."

"Well, I don't give a rat's ass—" He tried to pull away from Chiun, but the old man gripped his arm tightly.

"Think, Remo! For once, will you think? Jilda is of an ancient people. They would never accept you as one of them, and so you would live apart, as outcasts. She would bend her ways to yours, because she is a woman, and that is their nature. But she would miss her home, and her people, and the old ways in which she was reared. In time, she would grow to resent you. Perhaps even hate you."

"Nope," Remo said. "Not that one. She wouldn't care. Besides, I'd make up for it. For God's sake, I'd do anything for her."

"It would not be enough. And you, my son, who are so eager to throw off your responsibilities to Sinanju. Without you, there will be no Master of Sinanju after me. Except . . ."

Suddenly Remo understood. "The Dutchman," he said.

"And while the Dutchman wields his power, unchecked, your abilities will have diminished beyond help through lack of use. Why do you think I have you work for Emperor Smith? You are still growing in the ways of Sinanju. You must work for many more years before you may take my place as reigning Master. But after even one year of idleness—or what you think of now, in your dreams, as happiness—all I have taught you will be gone. You cannot rest, any more than the Dutchman."

Remo could still hear the distant waves lapping on the shore. "Did you talk Jilda into leaving me?"

"I said nothing. She is not stupid. Nor am I willing to force you to accept the destiny of Shiva as your own. But you must know the truth. That is why I have broken my promise to Jilda. If you go to her now, at least you will go with some understanding of the consequences.'' He released Remo's arm and walked away.

Remo stood very still. The sea called to him. Green and blue and gray, the colors of Jilda's eyes. Soon there would be a child, Remo's child, with the same strange, unworldly gaze. A beautiful child, born of a love and passion that would never be duplicated.

A child for the Dutchman to find and kill . . .

Remo covered his face with his hands. It would happen, he knew. The Dutchman would never be sane. In his search for death, he would surely come for Remo, because he understood now that their lives were permanently enmeshed. And Remo would have weakened. Even if he practiced the exercises of Sinanju every day, he would not have Chiun to guide him.

It would be so easy, with Jilda and the baby, to forget the Dutchman altogether. A peaceful life, quiet, comfortable. But one day the Dutchman would come back for him. And Jilda. And the child. The beast inside him would see that Remo had no heirs.

He whispered, ''Jilda, I can't do it.''

But she had known that all along, he realized.

He turned, cold inside, from the sound of the waves and walked back to Chiun. The old man was waiting for him.

''I wonder if I'll ever see the baby,'' he said.

''Do you think you could bring yourself to part with them then?''

Remo thought. ''No. No, I guess not.'' They walked a long way. ''Never, then.''

''Jilda is a fine woman. She will raise a good son.''

''Or daughter,'' Remo said. ''I've always wanted a daughter.''

"A son," Chiun said simply.

"What makes you so sure what it'll be?" A thought occurred to him that made him feel as if his heart had just shot into his throat. "Not another one of your crazy legends."

"Some traditions must be continued," Chiun said, walking ahead.

"Oh, no. No kid of mine is going to go through this. I won't let it happen."

Chiun turned and smiled. "Then you do believe, after all."

Remo scowled. "You old conniver," he said, strolling beside him.

Jilda. Oh, Jilda, how I'll miss you.

It was a clear night, a night of beginnings and endings. Somewhere on a starlit sea a child was growing. And here, a world away, Remo was alone. Again. It broke his heart.

"I wish . . ."

"Yes?"

"It doesn't matter."

"Go ahead. Sometimes it helps to talk."

Remo swallowed. "I wish things didn't have to turn out the way they do."

Chiun put his arm around him. "I know, my son," he said gently. "I know."

Remo felt in his pocket. His carved jade stone from the Master's Trial was still there. He clutched it tightly. It was all he had to remind him.

His eyes filled. "Go on without me," he said. The old man walked ahead. When Remo was alone, he turned his face to the trunk of a tall tree and wept. For himself, for Jilda, for the child he would never see. The Golden Lady would never be his until the day he died. All he had left of her was a cold jade stone.

A breeze cooled his face, carrying with it the faraway scent of the sea. He looked up. Not all. He had something else, after all. For among the thousands of stars gleaming in the summer sky, one shone above all the others. Gullikona, with its golden fire, burned only for him.